The Captain's Log

Hans Mateboer

ISBN 0-9749915-9-7

Contents

Introduction

Writing is a very fascinating process. Playing with words and sentences in such a way that they fit together, is not an easy task at all. Numerous books have been written about the sea and those who sail on her, but extremely rare is a book written by a seaman himself.

Our minds are not trained to sit behind a computer to endlessly toy with words. Instead, they are shaped by North Atlantic storms, hurricanes and shifting cargos. In our dealings with people from all over the world, the quality of English language we often use, would be severely frowned upon by any self respecting Kindergarten teacher.

Seamen in general are experts in expressing themselves clearly in very few and simple words and often a plain gesture is deemed sufficient. Thus, the sea has prepared us to deal with all kinds of situations fast and effectively. A high degree of bluntness is not uncommon.

That writing is not a quality associated with us, shows in the fact that I cannot think of any Captain who has written a book like this. I know very well from my own experience that a lack of material cannot be the reason for it. I believe that every person has his own fantasy world in which he achieves fantastic, if often impossible goals. It is the same with me. During my numerous night shifts being alone on a dark ocean, my imagination often would run wild. I would start shipping companies, I would write books…

A few times I actually made an attempt to do the last, but never got much further than the title. After all what would I write about…?

Then, some years ago, it occurred to me that I didn't have to torture my brain to find ideas for a book. The book was happening right around me, in plain sight on my own ship, almost everyday, enough to fill many volumes. The above then, would imply that every story is a true one. My answer to that can only be 'yes'.

Everything you will read has truly happened. Of course, certain changes were necessary to fit episodes together. Every now and then a chapter will consist of more than one story combined and in virtually all cases I altered the names of those involved. I do hope that you will derive as much enjoyment from reading this book, as I got from writing it and reliving these experiences.

The Start of a Career

Back in the late sixties and the early seventies, cruising was in its infancy. And only a small select group of visionaries grasped the opportunity and fashioned a new industry. Most people in those years agreed it was more the twilight years of a once proud Trans Atlantic Liner way of life on which the sun was setting fast. A small fledgling group of companies was hanging on and desperately tried to make a profit. Their hanging on, in most cases, was more for the sake of not being able to sell off their old ships, rather than the keen business sense of perceiving the better times to come. They used their old ships, dinosaurs, hardly suitable for cruising, that somehow had managed to escape the torches of the scrap yards where so many of their mates had met their end.

The general public was not yet aware that one of the greatest vacations could be found on the high seas and the cruise companies had no defined strategy on how to tell them. Not only were the potential passengers ignorant of this, but so were we, the seafarers. All we knew was that the days of the great Atlantic Liners were over and done with, thanks to companies like Boeing and Douglas.

Our knowledge of the cruise lines was limited to the fact that they were steadily losing money. A sort of animosity even existed against the few officers who had remained sailing these big white ships. They sure had to be sissies and must hate honest work. Outcasts from the society of mariners they were, daring to live a life of luxury that had nothing to do with real ships.

Sometimes while I was on cargo ships we met them. During the day, their high spotlessly painted white hulls, visible from many miles distance, or at night, lighted up like Christmas trees. Standing on the bridge of my rusty old workhorse, I kept looking at them through my binoculars with a mixture of curiosity and hostility. Trying to spot girls in bikinis, sipping their drinks at the pool bar. Girls we sorely missed, and they were always the subject of our discussions during off duty hours, after we had met one of those ships. I kept watching, straining my eyes, till only a smoke plume could be seen over the horizon. I would never work on these ships, having to dress up all the time, hosting complete strangers at the dinner table, dancing till late at night. No sir, not me, I was a seaman.

Unlike most other children, already at a young age, I knew what I wanted to be, Captain and nothing else. This certain knowledge, strangely enough gave me an edge over the other kids, as there never was any doubt. In my little town, I was given credit for being an authority on the subject of the seas, based on my insatiable appetite for books about ships and mariners. Nobody, and certainly not me, realized that books about the voyages of James Cook and the adventures of Caribbean pirates hardly add to the creation of an authority on modern day shipping and most definitely do not prepare one adequately for a life at sea.

It must have been galling to my mother that this little whim of mine would not go away with the years.

"What do you want to be son?"

"Captain on a ship sir."

Invariably a smile would appear; after all what kid does not want to be a sea captain at one stage of his life? My mother always smiled proudly and agreed. Would not any parent go along with her five year old son's dreams? Over the years her benevolent smile slowly turned into one of slight alarm when my answers did not change, but after so many years of agreeing, she could not easily back out anymore. A few times she actually made some half-hearted attempts to change my interest into different fields.

Once when I showed some interest in chemical engineering, she bought me a big box filled with small bottles and glass tubes. 'A Chemical Kit for Children age 12 to 14' it said on the cover. Mother would dearly regret her present. Not only her tactics didn't work, it also cost her a new tablecloth and a carpet, as my concoctions were not as harmless as the cover of the box promised they would be. A few years later she was not above scheming with a few prospective girlfriends who clearly preferred a plumber or a carpenter to warm them during cold nights, to a captain away from them for months at a time. Nothing worked, and I went to Nautical College to prepare for a career on ships.

I went to sea when I was nineteen years old. An apprentice filled with school knowledge that had been all important when preparing for my exams. All too soon I made the painful discovery that much of it was rather useless in real life. In fact I barely knew port from starboard and in general was very ill prepared for the life that awaited me on that rusty old freighter which I boarded in the port of Rotterdam. Mother brought me to the ship, the trunk of her Ford filled with suitcases she had supervised packing, with contents of which I was not at all sure. Her eyes showed more and more alarm as we drove through the harbor area trying to find the ship and at the same time avoiding forklifts and trucks. Traffic rules so carefully adhered to in normal life did not seem to exist behind the gates we just passed.

My first trip would bring me to West Africa, to places with exotic names like Sierra Leone and Ivory Coast. Little did I realize that the days of the great steamship lines were almost over, and the ship I was boarding, was a relic from the past that had outlived itself already by a good many years. To me the 'Freetown' although rather rusty, was the start of a new life, a life I had been looking forward to ever since I could remember.

Climbing the long wobbly gangway with only a few ropes as handrail was a dangerous undertaking, certainly when carrying two suitcases filled with everything my mother could think of. Packing them, had taken me a good deal of talking to convince her that the selection of small mirrors and colored beads she insisted I should bring, would not save me from a tribal cooking pot as they had done with various missionaries during times long gone.

"You idiot, are you trying to kill yourself!"

I stopped in my tracks and balancing somewhere halfway up I looked behind me, trying to figure out who the idiot could be that the uniformed man at the top of the gangway was yelling at. There was nobody behind me. To my consternation, he started running down the plank, causing it to sway dangerously. Did he want to pass me on that narrow thing? That was impossible. Before my thoughts could progress any further, the man reached me and grabbed me by my collar with his left hand, while with his other, not too kindly, he took one suitcase from me. A few minutes later we reached the deck of the ship where I received a dressing down, I will not lightly forget. The bearded man appeared to be the Chief Officer of the 'Freetown', who I later learned possessed a kind and caring heart, but whose verbal expressions and opinions about mankind in general would indicate the total opposite.

The man I met that first minute was the prototype of the seamen I would get to know so well during all those years at sea. Introvert, rough with words, often very explicit in their choice of them to voice disgust, but so generous with help and always ready to assist the very creatures they disliked. I soon learned that the lowest form of life, were those living ashore and having a 9 to 5 job. A particular disgust often was voiced about those anonymous souls who worked at the head office. According to what I heard, these people were never there when needed. This, according to the speakers was just as well, as during the rare occasions when they were available and tried to help, it usually went wrong anyway.

The seamen I sailed with over the years on cargo ships, were often a rough lot, not afraid of anything it seemed, especially not when one listened to them during after work hours, sitting at the ship's bar behind an ever-increasing amount of empty beer glasses.

During those first weeks on the old 'Freetown' I listened to them, red-eared, taking it all in and marveling about this strange world I had entered. A world of fantasies about women and strange adventures in exotic ports, about hurricanes, shifting cargos and North Atlantic gales.

After more than 25 years at sea, now I know that most of the stories I was told and believed at that time must have been a compilation of many happenings. Adventures that had reached the teller, not through his own experience, but via a neighbor at a bar somewhere in the world, who in turn, most likely also had heard it from somebody else.

I was unpacking my suitcase in a tiny cabin with a desk, a bed, a window and just enough space to turn around, provided the chair was under the desk, when suddenly bells started ringing and the ship's whistles started to blow. Having successfully passed the exams at the Nautical College I was sure there had to be some meaning to all this noise, but I simply could not guess what it was. Making a fool of myself had already happened once that day and doing so twice was clearly inadvisable. After all, the gentleman at the gangway had told me that he never wanted to see me again if I kept doing such stupid things. He had used terms totally unfamiliar to me, and it would be many months before I even vaguely would begin to understand them. It was clear however, that they referred to my whole family, the quality of modern day education and my appearance in general.

Hurriedly I pulled out my brand new uniform and put it on, fumbling with the tie. A few days before, I had pictures taken in it, my mother very proud, wanted to show off to the neighbors and friends. A few kids playing nearby had been very impressed when I appeared in the garden followed by my mother clicking away on her old Kodak. Now wearing it again I felt less sure of myself. Gone were the admiring glances of the neighborhood kids and gone was the respect of the junior students at the academy for their seniors ready to leave for sea.

Finding the navigation bridge only took me about thirty minutes and when entering I found myself in surroundings that looked rather unfamiliar. Without doubt however, I had arrived at the right place. Charts, clocks, brass lamps, an enormous wooden steering wheel exactly as I had expected to see and an array of mysterious instruments. A small group of men, obviously the officers, going by their uniforms, were standing in front of a window, staring outside with their backs to me. One of them with four gold stripes on his shoulder boards, the Captain.

At the academy, the teachers had told us about the officers we would meet and how we were expected to behave. Whenever they talked about the Captain, they always lowered their voices and told us students that this was an almost god-like figure with dictatorial powers. A man to be friends with, and certainly not to be crossed!

I had forgotten that when entering, the door to the navigation bridge had needed considerable force to open, as apparently a formidable door closer was installed.

WHAM!!!

A gun fired next to me, could not have made more noise than the door slamming shut. I almost died right there and so did the four men with their backs to me. The Captain spilled most of the coffee from a cup he held in his hands over his starched white uniform. The Chief Officer, one of the four, recognized me and started another of his colorful descriptions, again including my family, but this time commenting on their actions going back as far as three generations. The Captain, mopping his uniform with a napkin, apparently was used to tirades like this and waited patiently for the Chief to finish, meanwhile looking at me like a farmer appraising his cattle.

"Who is that?"

"Our new apprentice sir."

"Looks even worse than the one we lost two months ago."

"I'll take care of him, don't worry."

"What's his name?"

"What's your name?"

"Hans Mateboer, sir."

"His name is Hans Mateboer."

"Has he been at sea before?"

"Have you been at sea before?"

"No sir, it will be my first trip."

"It's his first trip."

My mouth slowly had dropped open during this one sided conversation. I felt like a cow being sold at a market and at any moment expected the Captain to open my mouth to have a look at my teeth and check my health. Without saying another word or further acknowledging my existence he turned around and resumed his conversation with another officer, who, I later learnt, was the Chief Engineer.

A few hours later, a man with only one stripe on his shoulder and therefore much more human in my eyes, came to my cabin. He told me I was expected on the bridge, as we would depart in half an hour. Excitement rushed through my whole body; now it would happen, we would be leaving. My first voyage was about to begin. It was already dark when I arrived on the bridge, making the place look rather eerie. Tuned down lights of the instruments, the radar sweep casting shadows against the ceiling and against the faces of the men standing behind it. Looking out of the windows, I saw sailors casting off lines upon orders given through a radio by a man I took to be the pilot, as I had not yet seen him before. He was talking to our Captain about river currents and tugboats.

Looking closer, I saw two of them pulling the 'Freetown' slowly off the pier and into the river, where they cast off. We were on our own and underway to West Africa. I looked around at the lights of the refineries and the city and the factories along the banks, the lights of the incoming and outgoing ships and listened to the constant chatter on the radio.

I can still relive those hours as if they happened yesterday, and I believe that they were not much different than what any man new to the sea would experience today. I can't remember how long I stood there, mesmerized by the scenery and the atmosphere, taking it all in, feeling like being in heaven, when suddenly I was roughly disturbed by the Chief Officer. I started to dislike the man.

"You there, go on deck and help prepare the pilot ladder, he will be leaving in 15 Minutes."

"The pilot ladder, where do I go?"

He vaguely waved with his hand, indicating a general position somewhere in front of us.

Looking into the darkness on the deck below, I could distinguish a wide variety of equipment, most likely all part of the cargo. Tractors, trucks, crates and drums and somewhere in that confusing array must be the pilot ladder.

Finding my way to the deck below proved to be surprisingly easy and I collected my thoughts feeling a little surer of myself. At school we had learnt how to prepare this ladder, hang it overboard, so the pilot could climb down into a small boat to leave the ship. At school however, we always had done this during daytime with a lot of other students to assist and at a leisurely pace. Never on a dark deck, clogged with every imaginable piece of equipment the western world had to offer to the lesser-developed countries. Never with the help of only one sailor, who at first, in the dark I could hardly see.

His name was Moses, and while we struggled to get the ladder in place, he told me he was from Sierra Leone in West Africa. Moses was a good man and talking to him, I received some badly needed nice words, the first ones during that day. Slowly we lowered the ladder over the side, me holding it, while Moses watched how much further it had to go before it was in position.

"Five more feet."

I had to shift my grip on the rope to another part and in the dark, blindly grabbed around me to find it, there it was.

"Hey, what are you doing, hold it!"

To my horror, I heard a rumbling sound, then a splash and saw Moses leaning far overboard, both his hands in the air, watching something disappear in the wake of the ship.

"Man, look what you did, you lost the ladder."

Perplexed I looked at the rope I was still holding in my hand. It wasn't part of the pilot ladder. It was one of the safety lines instead. Slowly I dropped it. In the dark, with my inexperienced eyes, every rope looked the same, and I had thought… Horror stricken, my thoughts focused on the immediate future of having to face the Chief Officer, with only one consolation that without a ladder he could hardly send me home. Moses stared at me, his eyes wide with amazement.

"It's the first time we ever lost a pilot ladder and we only have one. Man, oh Man, you better go up and tell them."

"You did what???" Four pairs of eyes looked at me, the captain, the Pilot, the Chief Officer and the Third Officer. The latter barely able to conceal his delight as finally somebody had arrived on board who clearly would catch most of the abuse in the future.

I can't remember how it all ended. I was not fired on the spot or even keelhauled. The incident however followed me for years to come, as I was the one who had lost a pilot ladder. Something, which had never happened before in the hundred-year history of the company.

What I do remember however, is that upon going to bed that evening my confidence about a career at sea had disappeared completely. I seriously doubted the fact that I ever would be a true seaman.

The First Cruise

After years of sailing on rusty old cargo ships to every imaginable destination in the world, I decided that enough was enough. My old company, proud and arrogantly resisting any change and looking down upon all those newer and more aggressive outfits from Liberia and Panama, had ceased to exist. For the last two years I had sailed for a variety of companies, some employing me for as short as three weeks. The living conditions on board also were ever deteriorating as every company seemed to be struggling to make ends meet. I could not see myself going on like this and a future at sea for a young guy like me seemed bleak.

During a period ashore, studying for my Masters license, I met an old friend who worked for a cruise line. Compared to us freighter boys, he seemed to be a man of the world, a true dandy he was, and talked about his life on cruise ships like it was paradise. One exotic port after another was mentioned, which to us, used to crummy cargo piers far away from any civilization sounded like Utopia. To be honest, what most appealed to me, were his stories about a seemingly unlimited supply of beautiful women, apparently all single and all looking for a dashing man in uniform.

Frequently I found myself dreaming away during our lessons, seeing myself on board a cruise ship, surrounded by admiring girls in bikinis.

"Do they need any officers?"

"Oh yeah, they are expanding the fleet and I think you should talk to them."

I made a decision then and there to give this a try. One could always return in case the stories were not true.

Two weeks later, I found myself talking to Mr. Trevor, a man in his early fifties, Director of Human Resources, for the Continental Cruise Line, a renowned company that, I later learnt, was desperately trying to survive the transition to cruising and one, that was not too successful in its attempts at that time. Mr. Trevor of course did not mention this to me; instead he painted a rather rosy picture of the future, as apparently his company had taken over a competitor of many years. Being a gullible job applicant, I of course did not realize that the takeover was more a bank forced merger between two nearly bankrupt companies, and of course believed Mr. Trevor. He even mentioned 'Economies of Scale', a term which nowadays has become very fashionable and which I must have heard a million times ever since, but which at that time was a novel one and bound to impress people.

"So you work on cargo ships, which company if I may ask?"

Mentioning the word 'cargo ships', I noticed that Mr. Trevor's left cheek pulled back a little much in the same way one often sees when somebody looks at tasteless food. I started to feel a little uncomfortable, that the interview was going the wrong way and that nothing I could do or say would improve the situation. When I mentioned the name of my present employer, Mr. Trevor made a face as if I had said a very dirty word.

"Rather unacceptable I would say."

I heard him muttering. While he made a few notes on a piece of paper, his left hand cupped his mouth, displaying utter disgust and almost unperceivable, he moved his chair a little away from me. My heart sank, realizing that I would not be hired and that my dreams would remain dreams after all. Well, so what? I did not need this guy and his precious company. Until now I had been able to make a perfectly good living without them. Before Mr. Trevor could say good-bye to me, already having taken his handkerchief out of his pocket, to wipe his hand after my handshake, the telephone on his desk rang.

"Trevor."

It took a while before the person on the other side of the line stopped talking.

During this conversation, which was totally one sided, Mr. Trevor only nodded every now and then, but each time he did so, his face fell, until finally it looked like an approaching tropical depression. Finally he was ready to say something, but apparently had some trouble collecting his facilities as his Adam's apple was bobbing up and down as if trying to swallow a bite too big.

"What?" He's quitting because his wife found out about a few little affairs! I don't believe it. I keep telling them to be a little more discreet. Wives should not be allowed on board, I tell you!"

Mr. Trevor slammed down the telephone and looked at me with menacing eyes.

For at least two minutes he did not speak, then with a visible effort he managed a sour insincere smile.

"Well, maybe you came at the right moment. It seems we might have an opening for a second officer on the 'Manhattan', but you will have to be ready in two days to join her in New York."

Driving home, the reality of what I had done suddenly hit me. I was going to sail on cruise ships, join a crowd I always had been all too negative about. My family however was ecstatic, for ulterior motives no doubt, as they did not show their enthusiasm until after I had explained the package of privileges I had received. Privileges, that included free cruises for immediate family members.

After two days of hurried good-byes, a shopping spree and a Trans-Atlantic plane ride, I found myself in Southgate Tower, a hotel in central New York. There were four of us, two engineers, me and the Captain, all to join the ship the next day. The latter was a gray haired gentleman smoking a pipe, reminding me more of my grandfather than of a man in command of a major cruise ship.

Early next morning a taxi brought us to the ship. For several minutes, I found myself standing on the dock, open-mouthed and with butterflies in my stomach, looking at the giant ship berthed in front of me. She had just arrived and her uniformed crew was busy tying her up and rigging gangways. The first thing I noticed was that she was clean, unlike all my past ships. On her no rust showed at all, despite the fact that she had to be a good twenty years old.

An officer wearing a cap approached me and disdainfully asked me if I was the new second. Mutely I nodded, impressed, as never before had I seen such a white uniform and certainly not with a matching cap. Oh yes, we did have uniforms on cargo ships too, used about once a year on special occasions. I was painfully aware that mine would not even remotely stand a comparison with what I saw in front of me, it having yellowed during years of neglect.

In awe and not a little confused, I followed him through a maze of corridors, an elevator and corridors again. A panic slowly rose inside me; surely I would never be able to find my way around in this floating labyrinth. I saw hundreds of people, sitting in staircases, luggage scattered around them, waiting to leave the ship I assumed. Wild thoughts flashed through my mind, I could still leave, just walk off the ship and disappear, find a cargo ship and sail happily ever after. Just turn around and flee. Then I realized the utter futility of this, as I would never be able to find my way out alone. Discouraged I followed the other guy.

After what seemed like an eternity we arrived on the navigation bridge, where a bunch of officers, more than I had ever before seen together on one ship, were sitting around a table drinking coffee. They all looked at me, curiosity in their eyes. It was obvious that I had been the topic of their conversation right before as well as now. A new guy, joining from another company was virtually unheard of in those days. Nowadays with the international cruise fleet growing at an enormous rate, it is common enough to hire from outside. Me being one of the first explained the reaction of Mr. Trevor too.

I was told to put my belongings in my cabin and report back to the bridge in full uniform right after lunch. Lunch, by the way, was served in the Lido I was told. A young apprentice who effortlessly found his way around showed me to my cabin, with which I was pleasantly surprised. A desk, a nice sofa, a double bed, toilet and shower, everything was there and compared to most cargo ships I sailed on, it was very clean. I sat down on the bed, my panic slowly disappearing. If an apprentice could find his way around, surely

I could too, even to a place called 'the Lido'

My battered suitcase appeared meager compared to the three steamer trunks and four big boxes standing in the corridor. They belonged to the guy who had just vacated my cabin, going home to make peace with his narrow minded wife. While unpacking my uniform, I looked at it, with its tattered gold stripes, green with decay and exposed to a thousand storms and rain showers. I felt a little awkward wearing it and was not sure at all if I should wear the cap as well. I left it in my cabin. My search for the 'Lido' had started.

Forty minutes later I sat down on a sofa, my hair wet with sweat, completely confused about my whereabouts. I recognized that sofa too. I had passed it at least three times.

"Where is the 'Lido' young man?"

"Uh, what?"

A woman in her late sixties had stopped; she was dressed in a blouse with the top three buttons open and in a pair of shorts, that I would have loved, had they been worn by a girl of my age. Her eyes went over me appraisingly and she repeated her question.

"I don't know, was looking for it myself, just joined the ship today."

"Oh, very good, let's look for it together then, I'm hungry."

The way she kept staring at me, made me a little uncomfortable specially so since I was not very sure what she meant. For a moment my discomfort even turned into slight alarm, when she took my hand and started pulling me out of the sofa, allowing me a generous look into the interior of her blouse. Then I hear footsteps behind me.

"Mother, where have you been, we were looking for you all over the ship, Peter is waiting in the 'Lido'."

A beautiful girl, a few years younger than me, had come running down the staircase behind us. My mouth opened and closed again, unable to speak as I stared at her. She was exactly the girl I dreamt about, the type cruise ships were supposed to be filled with. My spirits lifted considerably and I looked at her mother with different eyes.

"I met this nice young man, we were just on our way to the 'Lido'."

Careful not to take the lead, I followed Amanda, as that was her name, to the 'Lido', all the while talking to her and her mother like I had been on cruise ships all my life.

"Maybe you can join us for lunch."

Mother, who I later learnt, carried the romantic name of 'Meg', asked. Thinking about the wonders, that were in store for me during my first trip on a cruise ship, I happily agreed. And what a cruise it could be, if only I could cultivate my relationship with Amanda and Meg a little more. All the unbelievable stories about women on board cruise ships seemed to be true after all.

At the 'Lido' we met a guy, who to my intense relief, was only the brother of Amanda, and not some 'lowlife' of a boyfriend. He was as friendly as could be and both Amanda and Peter seemed to adore Meg, who to me was very nice. She patted my knee repeatedly and moved a little closer each time, until I started regretting that I took a sofa to sit down on and not a single chair at the other side of the table. Of course I pretended not to notice.

We chatted as if we had known each other forever and Amanda told me she had broken up with her boyfriend a few months before, an act I secretly applauded. She was not looking for somebody else yet she said, looking me straight in the eyes. I couldn't believe my good luck and leaned over the table towards her, while Meg leaned over to me. A little annoying of course, but once at sea, she would realize it was her daughter I was after.

I did not see the Chief Officer coming until he stood in front of our table. His face showed complete surprise seeing me with this beautiful girl, obviously having a good time. In utter amazement he exclaimed; "I thought you were told to report to the bridge after lunch! Instead I find you chasing girls. You're fast, I give you that, but it's hardly a good start being on board only a few hours and already out of line."

I was dumbfounded, what had I done wrong? I looked at my watch and with horror saw that it was 3pm already, long past the reporting time. A feeling of doom came over me and I started to get up, but the Chief had left already. This didn't look good, my first day on the job and reprimanded already. At least, looking at Amanda, chances were good that it would be worth it. Getting up and looking at them, I managed a smile. Meg grabbed my arm.

"I will see you during the cruise I hope, maybe you can visit my cabin sometime soon."

I immediately agreed, the prospect of visiting Amanda, at least made the idea of having to face the Chief Officer bearable.

"Alright, but I have to go now, otherwise I'm in trouble. What's your cabin number?"

"Cabin 371."

Amanda and Peter also got up; both hugged Meg and kissed her on both cheeks.

"Hope you have a terrific cruise Ma, we have to go, they just announced visitors ashore."

"What? You are not coming on this cruise?"

My voice was shrill with consternation, what was this, had they brought their mother to the ship only, and I had thought...

"Oh, we are so happy that we met you, first we thought Mother would be lonely, but now you can keep her company."

Amanda and Peter vigorously shook my hand expressing their gratitude. Amanda even went as far as giving me a kiss and hugging me. She looked at me strangely, as I suddenly must have seemed lukewarm, as all enthusiasm had drained away. Not very successfully trying to smile, I promised them their mother would not be alone.

On the navigation bridge, the Chief Officer hardly acknowledged my presence and instead loudly announced his opinion about me to the Captain. The grandfather figure of yesterday had turned into a man with penetrating gray eyes, which seemed to bore straight through me. Both snorted and turned their backs.

Buster

"You are also invited, and don't you find any excuses!"

The captain pointed at me with his finger, the moment I had entered the navigation bridge. His voice betrayed a high degree of agitation and I saw that he had spilled some of his coffee, as he was in the process of wiping up a puddle from the windowsill. The Chief Officer was standing next to him, very red in the face. It seemed to me that either he had received a severe dressing down, or that he was barely able to keep from laughing out loud.

Until that day, the Captain had barely spoken two words to me and I felt honored that he was including me in his invitation. Although, I did not have a clue as to what this invitation was all about. He turned around to face the Chief Officer again.

"Don't you laugh!"

He said to the Chief Officer hotly.

"I didn't even realize that she was on board. Should have expected her anytime though, she hasn't taken a cruise in over a month. Still I wouldn't mind if she stayed home."

He seemed very annoyed and he spilled some coffee again without even noticing it.

"That woman drives me nuts, always parties, always wanting all the attention, and always it's me she's after"

"'Noblesse oblige' sir."

The Chief Officer volunteered. The Captain stared at him for a few seconds and snorted.

"Spare me your quotes, you probably got them from your

calendar anyway."

He turned around again towards me.

"Be ready in your formal uniform, at seven sharp, right here. The Purser, the Hotel Manager, the Chief Engineer, me, are all invited to a private party and you are coming as well."

"What kind of party sir?" I asked. "Do we have to bring something?"

"No, you just come along."

After the Captain had left, I looked at the Chief Officer and the Navigator on duty, who as soon as the door had closed burst out laughing. The Chief Officer even laughed so hard that he had to steady himself on the radar. I had been looking forward to attending parties, a part of cruise ship life I yet had to sample. This however must be different, something was wrong here, too much laughter and why was the Captain so upset?

"What's going on here?"

The only answer I got was more laughter; the Chief Officer started to gasp for air.

"Oh man, haven't laughed like this for a long time. What did you say?"

I repeated my question, very curious now about this party, which seemed to unsettle everybody by just mentioning it.

"It's a birthday party of our passengers and she invited almost all the officers. All except me, because she doesn't approve of me."

Again the Chief Officer started to laugh.

"Nobody can refuse to go because she owns a zillion shares in the company and can be as mean as poison, and she always gives these parties."

I started to become a little annoyed, everybody kept mentioning parties, but so far the funny part about it kept eluding me. I have never been a man thriving on going from one social affair to the other, but on the other hand, a good gathering every now and then I do enjoy. What was so funny?

"So what's wrong with her celebrating her birthday, it seems perfectly normal to me."

An explosion of fun erupted again. The Navigator reached for a big red handkerchief from his pocket and started wiping the tears from his eyes. The Chief Officer lifted his and, indicating that he was more or less ready to tell me more about the joke.

"Marge Winkler is one of our faithful passengers. She makes about 20 cruises a year and always at this time she celebrates a birthday. We all have known her for years and every year she looses it a little more. Not to say, she is stark raving mad! She wants all officers to come to that birthday party and nobody can refuse, because she will find you."

It all was becoming a little childish I thought. To me it seemed rather normal that a group of officers was required to attend a private party. I was just about to inform the Chief Officer of my thoughts, when he resumed his story.

"The funny part is that it isn't her birthday at all, it's her Teddy Bear's. His name is Buster."

Suddenly I started to smile, visualizing the whole scene already. Joining the laughter, I actually started to look forward to seven o'clock.

Ten minutes before time I was on the bridge. For the first time in my life dressed in a formal uniform with a collar so stiff I thought it would choke me. One by one the other officers came in, all dressed similar and none of them looking too happy. With a certain amount of apprehension, I followed them through the corridors, the Captain in front, to one of the most expensive suites on board the ship. Being the first, the Captain loudly knocked on the door and waited. After about two minutes, slowly the door was opened and an elderly lady looked at us with uncomprehending eyes.

"Hello Ma, we are here for the party, it's Buster's birthday remember."

"Oh yes, of course, come in but be careful, he is still asleep."

We all moved in, followed by a few stewards pushing carts with drinks and appetizers. Never having been in these state-rooms, I looked around curiously. The cabin was huge, beautifully decorated and about ten times the size of my own, which I already thought to be very spacious. In a corner stood a queen size bed in which a body laid, covered with blankets and propped up with pillows. Sticking out above the covers, I saw the head of a big Teddy Bear. This must be Buster! Startled by an un-expected sound I turned around and saw Ma Winkler. She was sobbing and tightly holding the arm of the Captain with one hand. Our Commander looked decidedly embarrassed and I moved a little closer to hear what was being said.

"Oh, it's all my fault. I insisted since it was his birthday. He so strongly disapproves of me drinking Bloody Marys for lunch and dinner. He never drinks them you know, only Virgin Marys. Now he's sick because I put a shot in his drink. He threw up you know. I have to give up these drinks, if only for him. By the way, would you like one?" She asked turning around to me.

Never having liked the drink I started to refuse, but when I looked around me, I saw every single person in the room holding a glass of the red stuff. The stewards had brought nothing else but it. Without waiting for my answer, she put a glass in my hand and pulled me over into a corner. In the background I saw big grins of relief appearing on the faces of the Captain and the other officers, somebody else was singled out.

"What's your name young man?"

Without even listening to the answer, she came over even

closer and started to whisper in my ear, every few seconds looking furtively behind her as if afraid somebody else would want to listen in on this privileged conversation.

"You seem to be very intelligent to me and I have to tell you something."

By now she held my head with both her hands, one at the nape of my neck, and the other under my lower jawbone, making me feel rather uncomfortable. I tried to move away, but Ma was surprisingly strong. The others by now were enjoying the party very much and looked at Ma and me with unconcealed delight.

"Buster is not a real man at all." She whispered. "He is just a Teddy Bear! They all think he is real you know and I can't bear breaking the truth to them, they are all so nice. Oh! Look, he is waking up. He wants to get out of bed!"

Abruptly letting me go, she moved over to the bed, uncovered the bear and carried him to a chair. Buster appeared to be an early specie, his fur was all but gone and at various parts of his ancient body I saw pieces of straw stuffing sticking out.

"Well, are you not going to wish him a happy birthday?"

Ma expectantly looked at the officers huddled together in a corner of the cabin and pointed at the Captain.

"You are the first one."

With a 'devil may care' look on his face he moved over and took Buster's right paw in his hand and shook it vigorously.

"Congratulations Buster."

The other officers including me followed and Buster took all the good wishes quietly and in good nature.

"Yes, you too."

Ma Winkler looked at the Purser who so far had escaped all the attention and who during the course of the party had focused more on the cart with Bloody Marys than on Buster, and who as a result was none too steady on his feet. Smiling, he abided her wish and shook Buster's paw like we all had done. This time however the result was a little different from the previous times. Maybe it was the strong handshake of the Purser, it also could have been the result of hundreds of strong handshakes during parties like this before. Without any of us really noticing what happened, we were all startled by an anguished cry from Ma Winkler and an exclamation of surprise from the Purser.

Buster's right paw had come off at the shoulder joint, and he sadly sagged to one side of the chair.

"A doctor! Quick, do something!"

Ma Winkler hysterically pounded the Captain on his chest, who not expecting such a sudden attack staggered into a corner like a boxer losing the match. It was unnerving to see the sudden change in the old lady, still banging away at the Captain, her tidy hair becoming undone.

"Do something." The Captain snapped at the ship's doctor who until now happily had followed the scene, escaping all attention. The man's mouth dropped wide open.

"Who, me?"

"Yes you, you're the doctor aren't you?"

"Please help my little Buster." Ma Winkler wailed. "He's in pain, can't you see that!" It was obvious that the physician did not have enough fantasy to cope with the situation, not even after the Purser had unceremoniously dropped the severed paw in his hands. By now we all started worrying if Ma wasn't the one needing a doctor. She looked deadly pale and allowed the Captain to lead her to the bed where she shakily sat down. At this moment the Captain firmly took control of the situation showing the leadership only a true Captain could display. "Call the upholsterer, on the double."

It took only a few minutes before the upholsterer arrived. He looked a little frightened at the assembled officers. None of them thought about leaving as soon as possible anymore. This party turned out to be very interesting. The little Filipino, not understanding the emotional damage he was inflicting, after he was explained what to do, stuffed the severed paw in his tote bag and carried Buster away, holding him by his leg.

Ma gave a piercing scream when she saw how her little darling was being handled, but the upholsterer was gone.

It took us a while to calm her down, and shakily she had two more Bloody Marys while we, in turn assured her that Buster would be fine. Not before long, Buster reappeared, his front paw where it belonged. Ma Winkler pressed the upholsterer to her heaving chest and showered him with sloppy kisses.

The party lasted another ten minutes before the Captain expressed his thanks to Ma and told her he was leaving, having to attend other duties. As we had come earlier that evening, we left, the Captain in front followed by his officers.

"You know what?" I heard him saying to the Chief Engineer. "The only normal one in that cabin, was that Teddy Bear." Ma Winkler died many years ago, but every now and then, hers and Buster's name still come up in our conversations. She was one of those passengers one does not easily forget, sometimes a pain, often a joy and always unforgettable.

Gone Fishing

Millions of people get their life's enjoyment out of fishing. Not me however. It has never been a favorite hobby of mine. I have tried it often enough and maybe it is because I'm not a very patient man and expect to see things happening at once, and at my time. I simply don't like sitting in a boat all day, waiting till some little fish gets it into his mind to bite. I often wonder what exactly it is that I don't 'get', when I sometimes see hundreds of people sitting at the side of a canal, just staring at the water. All these people must love to fish and so did our Captain...

Alaska is probably one of the greatest fishing locations in the world, and it is one of the things everybody seems to do there. Fishing, hunting, hiking and just about every thing else associated with outdoor life.

We had left Ketchikan a few hours before and were on our way to Juneau. It was a beautiful late afternoon and we sailed at full speed in an unforgettable landscape. Snow Passage, a very narrow stretch of water, requiring very careful navigation, was just an hour ahead of us. I had my binoculars ready, as this was a prime location to see some whales.

The Captain was standing to my left, in deep conversation with the Pilot. Of course, as always, when these two were together, it was all about fishing. How big a fish he had caught last week, what bait he used, how many hooks. All of which did not appeal to me. It was probably also the reason he never really talked with me that much, as our fields of interest were worlds apart.

"It's marvelous, I'll show it to you, just a minute." I heard the Captain saying, while he turned around and left the bridge.

We still had half an hour to go now till Snow Passage. I had called the engine room to warn the Engineers that I was going to slow down a bit to a speed that would allow the ship to be easier to maneuver. Necessary, when navigating in confined waters. After pouring himself a cup of coffee, the Pilot checked our position and course, concentrating on the coming narrow passage.

"Here it is, look, isn't it a beauty, just the feel of it in your hand. Bought it two days ago in Vancouver, a special order."

Both the Pilot and I looked behind us as the Captain came back on the bridge with a brand new fishing rod in his hands. Unlike me, the Pilot however showed more than only a fleeting interest. He turned around and gaped at the rod, the brand of which apparently was rare and top of the line. The Captain grinned, like a child in possession of a new toy.

"I'll show you. Look, you swing it and with a snap of your finger it releases. Never owned a fishing rod this accurate. You can get your bait exactly where you want it to go. Watch!"

While talking, the Captain swung the rod through the air, carefully avoiding the low ceiling. The accuracy indeed was impressive. Three hooks and a piece of lead hit a chair fifty feet away at the exact spot the Captain had predicted they would strike.

"Let me try it." The pilot almost grabbed the rod out of the Captain's hands. He reeled the line in, savoring the moment of holding such a fine piece of equipment in his hand.

"Man, it balances like a precision tool. All right, now I'll try to hit that chair too. Watch out"!

Balancing it, and ready to release, he swung the rod in wide arches. At the end of his last and widest swing he released the line so the lead could hit the same chair.

Anyone who has ever been on ships knows that the ceilings are not the highest, a fact that also applies to most Navigation Bridges. The Captain, having played with his toys on board often enough, was painfully aware of this restriction. He once had hit a sprinkler head and now allowed for this when he practiced. The Pilot however, used to the vast expanses of Alaska had never been in a fishing position where he had to take ceiling heights into account.

Exactly at the moment he released the line, the top of the fishing rod hit a smoke detector on the ceiling. This in itself was not the problem. The effect, however, diverted the lead and the three hooks with it into a totally different direction than was intended. It hit our Captain square on the head, which, the lead being only light, did no harm to him.

The real problem was that our good Pilot, the moment he saw what was happening, jerked the rod backward. An experienced fisherman later told me that this is the movement often used to hook a fish when one feels it nibbling at the bait. The same theory applied here. One of the hooks firmly embedded itself in the back of the collar of the Captain's shirt, the second one fell on the floor and the third one got solidly stuck in the seat of our Pilot's pants.

"We are getting very close to the passage now, maybe you should come over and check." I informed them, not yet aware of what had happened and what the complication was. Not getting any reply, I turned around to see what was happening, and it was a scene I will never forget. The Captain was on his hands and knees trying to get the hook unstuck from the Pilot's pants. While at the same time, the Pilot was bent over, plucking at the hook sitting in the Captain's collar. The other hook, the one sitting in the carpet, in the meantime, had significantly reduced their area of mobility to just a few feet.

"Sit still, or I'll never get it out."

"Me sit still, if you didn't keep moving I could get to your pants a lot easier."

"Ouch!!"

The Captain started sucking his finger, where the hook had cut into his skin.

"Sir, we are entering snow passage now, you better get over here."

Desperate to get loose, the Pilot yanked at the line, trying to pull it up from the carpet. The situation, however, was not at all clear with at least 50 feet of line lying around. In his haste, he had not really checked which end was attached to what, and his violent pull was applied to the wrong line. Our poor Captain almost toppled over backward by all that 'yanking power' applied to his shirt collar.

"Can you stop that, you fool! It's a three hundred pound line. Better get me some scissors from the chart room. You there, hurry."

The lookout, who, until now had silently observed the whole scene from a corner of the bridge, suddenly became the one to solve the situation. Startled into action, I heard him rumbling through some drawers.

"Where did you say they are? I don't see any."

That was the time when our good Captain decided that enough was enough. With a gargantuan effort he jerked against the line. One of the two hooks or just the line had to give way. The one embedded in the carpet held and so did the one in the collar of his shirt. The line didn't break either. Instead, with a tearing sound I saw him coming free, leaving the complete shirt collar behind. His neck red with the effort and with friction marks the shirt had left. At the same time, we entered Snow Passage, A few minutes later he turned around, as if nothing unusual had happened and spoke to the Pilot, asking him what he thought about the gear.

"I think you should get me those scissors. I'm still stuck to the floor and I didn't bring an extra pair of pants."

After having freed him, they kept talking for almost an hour, before the Captain finally went down to put on another shirt. He, nor the Pilot, ever seemed to think twice about what had just happened or even to mention it any further. Anything for their hobby! They were already making plans to go out fishing together later that week.

"We'll go out in my brother's boat when we get to Sitka. I know the best fishing grounds there. I bet we come back loaded with fish; Salmon, Halibut and you name it!"

It was all fine with me. As far as I was concerned, they could go fishing every day, as long as they stopped doing it on the bridge.

After we had anchored in Sitka a few days later, the Pilot, our Captain, and myself, were the first ones to leave the ship. I had shore duty on the pier, regulating the boats arriving from the ship with passengers. The other two were both loaded down with a whole collection of fishing equipment. Rods, tackle, bait, a big cooler straight from the ship's galleys, and a host of other items the purpose of which in most cases totally eluded me.

Shortly afterward, I saw a little worn out looking cabin cruiser leave the small harbor of Sitka. The plume of blue smoke, and the very few spots where the original blue paint still showed through on a rusty hull, told me that the pilot's brother was not into maintaining equipment to cruise ship standards. They disappeared behind the breakwater, and the last thing I saw was the Pilot digging into the cooler. Sitka is usually only a morning stop for cruise ships. Carrying all the passengers back and forth to the ship can be a very intense business. Needless to say I had not given any more thought to our Captain and his Pilot fishing friend.

Close to sailing time, our passengers always returned to the pier in droves, forming a long line waiting for a ship's tender to bring them back aboard. The line progressively grew to more than two hundred, a normal enough weekly occurrence.

'Puff...Puff...Puff...'

The cabin cruiser was returning to port. The Pilot behind the wheel and our Captain standing in front, a line in his hand, ready to moor the little craft. It was very obvious how excited he was about the catch. From more than a hundred feet away, he was already telling me about what a great morning they had and how much they had caught. The waiting passengers stretched their necks, as not to miss anything of what was being said. A few of them, obviously avid fishermen themselves, even joined in on the long distance conversation.

The Captain at this time looked around, then turned to the Pilot and said; "Hey man slow down or we're going to hit the dock." I saw the pilot stretching his neck from behind the wheel. His view obstructed by a collection of old lobster traps and other equipment on top of the cabin, and even more by the Captain himself. He fumbled with the controls.

"I can't see you're standing in my line of view. How far to go?"

"It's OK, just go slower to get her stopped."

Clearly the pilot misunderstood the Captain's words, and taking the word 'stop' a little too literally, he yanked the throttle back to full astern. The intermittent 'puffs' coming from the antiquated exhaust pipe increased to a heavy boost of black smoke. Whatever my earlier thoughts were about the state of maintenance of the little boat and her engine, I must admit, her stopping power was certainly not affected at all. Who really was affected, was our Captain. At the very front of the boat, he had just bent over to pick up a mooring line to throw to the dock, still 20 feet away. He uttered a startled cry, and with arms wildly flailing in the air he lost his balance disappeared into the black water of Sitka's harbor, head first.

There was total silence. Nobody uttered a sound. Our passengers, who had watched the approach with bored interest, were now holding their breath, eyes wide and mouths open in sheer amazement. The expression on their faces, however, changed in record time to one of equally sheer delight, when our Captain surfaced like a breaching whale, screaming: "Get me out of here, it's cold." Saving him bodily was done easy enough, but his pride was a different matter altogether. I think it drowned, right there in the dark depths of the harbor.

"You keep quiet about this."

Was the first thing he said when he stood there dripping on the pier in front of me. I readily promised I would. He turned around and got into an empty tender and told the driver to get him back to the ship. Wisely, I didn't suggest he share the boat with 50 or so waiting passengers. Based on his facial expression, this likely would have been a serious career diverter. My real dilemma was how to keep this quiet. Impossible, I thought! Two hundred passengers and a good number of crew had been spectator to this most unusual sight. I could just imagine that just about everybody was dying to share witnessing this first class entertainment event.

The cruise industry is a small community; and this was evident once again the same day when all kinds of funny messages started arriving on our poor Captain's desk. Messages from other ships, offering him a supply of life rings or inquiring about the Sitka harbor water temperature. We hardly saw him in public during that cruise, and only the most pressing matters could lure him from his cabin. I felt sorry for him when I heard him sneezing, but couldn't help myself from laughing and eventually sharing the story with others.

The Two Sisters

Going on a world cruise must be just about one of the most coveted ways of making a statement to the neighbors. Imagine the prospective travelers on tea gatherings throughout the world, or at the second hole at the golf course at the Country Club. Casually they drop the idea that they might not be around during next winter.

"We are thinking about doing something else, perhaps taking a 'World Cruise', hate the weather here, you know."

Remarks like this often are made to show off a little, the desired effect could be the opponent's golf ball ending in a sand trap or just to create envy. Casually making a remark about world cruising almost automatically puts the speaker in a different league.

Normal mortals don't do world cruises, even when taking a regular cruise has become a mainstream vacation. The world cruise still stands out as special, and rightfully so. The same goes for us as well, we all hope to be on the list of officers planned to be on board. I can still remember every single one I made. The privilege of being on board is usually preceded by some ferocious behind the screen scheming and a trading of favors.

"I wasn't planned last year, so it's about time to put me on."

We conveniently forget that the company has five or six other ships that need a crew as well. I will not tell you how many world cruises I've made, but I believe I have had my fair share of them, or not?

Every time again, it's amazing to see the passengers come on board, usually in New York, as a cruise like this should start there, it's tradition and nobody would want it otherwise. The far majority of those boarding, have done it before, traveling the world at leisure and know exactly what to expect. Often they even book the same cabin year after year. At first I could hardly believe the stories of people doing world cruises for more than once, but now I find it almost normal when meeting somebody who tells me, she has done it every year for the last twenty or so. Amazing is also the amount of luggage that is carried on board. Fifty or sixty pieces do not seem to be too excessive. Sometimes even a complete extra cabin is booked to be used for storage alone.

Watching people always has been one of my favorite diversions. Never do I complain when my wife feels the need to spend extended time walking around shopping malls or to fit new cloths in stores. I just sit down and wait and in the mean time watch with great curiosity.

Standing at the ship's gangway, greeting guests boarding or returning from a visit to another exotic port never has been a chore for me. It certainly was not, when embarking the passengers for my first world cruise now about 20 years ago. I had been cruising for almost five years and felt on top of the world. The immediate advantage of these five years, being the fact that I already knew a fair amount of the guests boarding.

Some of them would leave the ship three months later as friends while a few... well, a very few I would rather never see again. The far majority of the world cruise passengers are advanced in years, as who else would have the money and above all, the time to take off for a hundred days or more.

There is nothing more diverse in background than the passengers on a world cruise. Some are so generous, others tight as can be. There are the old ladies, dumped on the ship by their grateful children, just to get rid of Mom for a few months. There are the lottery winners and there are those who have saved for a lifetime to make this voyage. Not all are rich but most have fortunes of which most people only can dream about.

The arrival of some passengers is eagerly anticipated by the crew. To be honest, the reasons for this are usually selfish and go back to the basics, which is money. After all, when serving a select group of guests for three months in a row, it makes a huge difference for a steward if a particular person is generous or not. Not eagerly awaited in the least, were two sisters whom everybody already talked about before they even boarded. According to gossip they were fabulously wealthy, but unfortunately at the same time had a big aversion to sharing even the tiniest amount of their fortune with others.

A crew as a whole can be very cruel in their verdict and at the same time very funny in their ways to get a message across. Amongst ourselves we started to call them "Grisella and Anastasia in their very ripe age." Both names of course taken from the two stepsisters of Cinderella.

There are those people who will never be happy, no matter what they are doing and no matter where they are. At the same time they seem to reap some grim satisfaction from the fact that along the road they make life as difficult as possible for everybody else as well. Grisella and Anastasia were amongst this group.

Our voyage started on a freezing day early in January. The itinerary would bring us down the coast of South America, through the Straits of Magellan, the South Pacific and so on. I truly looked forward to it. After all how often does one make a grand voyage around the world and get paid for it too!

It wasn't until we sailed the straits of Magellan that I met Grisella for the first time. I was standing at the railing. The evening was breathtakingly beautiful. Snowcapped mountain peaks, behind which the sun had just gone down, giving them an incredible red and silver arch, surrounded us. The weather was crisp clear and clean. Suddenly a rasping voice next to me scattered the peace.

"Where are we?"

I turned around.

"Just about halfway through the Straits Madam."

And not able to remain silent about what I saw, I continued.

" Isn't this incredibly beautiful madam?"

"It's cold, we should be in nice weather."

She tapped the deck with her cane, making me believe she expected me to do something about it.

"Well madam, we are far south and it's normal to be a little chilly and…."

"Stupid answer, who are you anyway, I booked one of the most expensive suites on board and they sent me somebody like you, giving answers like that. I'll mention you to the Captain."

Open mouthed I watched her walking away, twice hitting an ashtray with her cane.

That she followed up on her promise I found out the next day, when I was called to the Captain's office.

"Please stay away from her if you can't tell her the things she wants to hear."

"But sir, I hardly said anything at all, she just assumed…

Waving his hand in an exasperated way, the Captain sighed.

"I know, I know, but then avoid her, it cost me twenty minutes this morning talking with her about your behavior and I have better things to do."

The voyage went on. We visited Kobe, Shanghai and many more places I had never been before. Then we passed Singapore and entered the Indian Ocean on our way to Madras and South Africa.

It was an early evening and I was just dressing for dinner when an announcement shook the peace on board. "Medical team, deck six forward!" Even though I was not part of any of this, I knew that something bad had happened, otherwise such an explicit announcement would not be made. As the location was close to my cabin, I decided to check if any help was needed, even if only by keeping the area clear of curious guests and crew. This turned out to be a good idea, as when I came around the corner into the announced area, I saw our senior doctor literally being attacked by Grisella, while Anastasia was lying on the floor.

"You fool!" she yelled at the top of her voice. "I'll get you for this!"

"Yes, but it appears she had a heart attack, I need to help her."

I assessed the situation immediately and put myself between Grisella and the Doctor, who immediately turned around and started administering help to the seemingly unconscious Anastasia.

With her fists, Grisella pounded my chest with amazing strength. "Look what the idiot is doing, he is damaging her jewelry! Watch that necklace, he could have broken it the way he took it off."

Wanting to stop her pounding, which at this stage was becoming rather painful, but at the same time not knowing how, was annoying. After all who likes to fight off a ninety year old woman who looks as frail as can be. Seeing the Security Officer arrive was the solution, as unlike me, he was paid to be a punching ball. Grisella didn't notice that now she was pounding a completely different person and kept ranting about broken jewelry and the cruise being a rip off. What she also didn't seem to see was that after a while the doctor sadly shook his head and got up.

To this day, I still cannot figure out if Grisella cared or not. When the body of her sister was carried away to the hospital, she kept making sure that every piece of jewelry was accounted for, even patting the pockets of some of the bystanders she suspected of having taken a ring she couldn't find.

Word of the incident got around very quick, Anastasia after all was well known by the passengers. Hadn't they made numerous World Cruises together? Nobody however seemed to think it too tragic an event. After all, at the age of over ninety, this event is not unnatural. Grisella's concern however was not so much with what arrangements to make, but more so with the associated cost. Anxious she inquired with the ship's purser what charges she could await and above all, how to reduce them.

We never figured out who, probably jokingly, mentioned to her that burials at sea would be free. What happened was that suddenly she started to nag our poor Captain that this was exactly what she wanted. Poor Anastasia even had mentioned this desire to her, she blatantly stated, and who were we to refuse her such a thing.

It took quite a few lengthy telephone calls with the head office of our company, before finally the Captain gave in to her wishes. After all why not, as there were no international rules forbidding us to do so. Seeing him on the bridge later on, grumbling, trying to put a service speech together was rather funny, even considering the circumstances.

At the same time, our ship's carpenters were busy, crafting a coffin. And to be honest, when I saw the result, I was impressed. Also the makeshift ramp was a piece of ingenious art. Erected in the luggage area, it had a cleverly constructed lever, that would, when pulled, release the coffin, which then through an open door, would slide into the sea. Our bosun, an experienced old salt, was in charge of the whole contraption and according to his own word, had dealt with similar situations numerous times.

Of course, we did not invite all the guests to the service, after all a luggage area is only so big. Only the closest friends were invited and it was amazing how many there seemed to be. Our purser, handling the requests to attend the service was less sure about the 'friend' part of it. While talking to the Captain, I overheard her stating that she believed that the invitees were more interested in a diversion on an otherwise normal day at sea, rather than in paying their respects.

The ceremony was to be held at 5 pm and the ship would slow down. The day before, the crew spent hours cleaning and painting the luggage area, an activity overdue anyway, and at 4 pm the coffin was brought up to be placed on the ramp. The bosun had it organized perfectly and nothing could go wrong. Carefully he directed his men to put it on the ramp and then opened the door so when ready there would be one smooth movement.

A few sailors brought in the podium, from which the Captain would lead the service and intended to put it next to the ramp. The bosun was still inspecting it and making some last minute adjustments. After all, he had bragged enough, stating his expertise, to let even the smallest detail interfere.

Maintenance on board a ship is an ongoing thing and often the engineers are swamped with work. All too often repairs in the passenger areas prevail above those needing to be done in those areas the guests normally never see. Sadly a situation like this had occurred again and a not so urgent repair had been postponed. The oil line, running from the hydraulic pump to the side door, that was opened to let the coffin slide through, had suffered from this neglect and even while the floor had been cleaned thoroughly, a small puddle of oil had formed on the steel deck.

"OK, lads put it there."

The bosun, directed his guys carrying the podium. Doing

one last step to position it, one of the sailors stepped in the small puddle and slipped.

"Oooh."

Desperately trying to keep his balance, he dropped the podium and stumbled backwards towards the slide. The poor man actually could have gone overboard through the opened door, had not the bosun been in his way.

"Hey, watch what are you're doing."

He yelled, when the staggering sailor bumped into him and in turn tried to keep his balance and stay away from the opened door. His hands mowed through the air, in search of something to hold on to and found the lever.

"Swoooosh…splash!…

"Oh my God!!"

After that, there was a silence while everyone, including me, rushed to the door to see the sinking coffin disappearing in the wake of the ship. The bosun, his face ashen, stared at some air bubbles indicating the location of where it was sinking to the bottom of the Indian Ocean. His mouth kept opening and closing, and for a while he was only able to make some gurgling sounds. It was clear that he had great difficulties expressing his true feelings. What he said when he was finally able to speak, I will not repeat, as it was rather unflattering for the sailor who had given him the shove, insulting even and very loud. But the same bosun also showed that during a lifetime at sea, a man could get used to making fast decisions

"Quick, close the door."

With one hand he started the hydraulic pump, while with the other he operated the handle used to close the door. After it had locked, without wasting any further words, he hit the hydraulic line with a crowbar. Oil poured onto the deck in front of us.

"Look what you did, you broke the pipe."

A slow thinking Engineer stammered. I, however marveled at the fast thinking of the bosun, this truly was a man of action and quick cover-ups.

"Why haven't you started yet, the casket should be here now. In ten minutes the guests will be here."

Nobody had seen the Captain arrive, his well-rehearsed speech in his hand.

"Oh, sir." The bosun wailed. "The pipe broke, we can't open the door, we left the coffin in the mortuary. We should postpone this until tomorrow. I told the technicians to fix it, days ago, but so far no action."

He continued in front of the Engineer, whose mouth dropped open, not able to process in is mind what his eyes and ears were telling him.

"Hmm, well, call it off then till tomorrow, it's always something on this ship."

Mumbling to himself the Captain turned around and left.

"You liar! You and your sailor pulled the handle and now you blame it on us. I'll tell the Chief, I'll...."

His hands in the air, the Engineer turned around to do what he had just promised to do."

"Yeah, go ahead, then I'll tell him that you are after that redhead passenger, and that I saw you in the nightclub with her last night."

With a visible effort the Engineer turned around and forced a smile on his face.

"Let's fix the pipe."

That night, the ship's carpenters worked overtime, how they did it, will always be a mystery, but the next day a brand new coffin stood ready, identical to the one we lost 400 miles back. The Engineer, the one illegally chasing the redhead, had provided some left over pieces of scrap iron to weight down the coffin to what he believed to be the correct weight.

Even after all these years I still feel a little guilty of not speaking up of what happened. On the other hand, the result of me doing so would have created a lot of problems. Maybe the Captain would even have decided to go ahead with the bosun's plan. We will never know.

The next day, again the area was cleaned and the guests gathered to pay their respects to their fellow passenger. The Captain did his speech and I saw that those few crewmembers standing around, who knew what really was happening, had great difficulties keeping their faces straight.

At the end, the Captain gave a signal for the Bosun to pull the lever, which he did for the second time in 24 hours. The coffin started sliding and when it tilted, we all heard a distinct rumbling inside, when the steel shifted to the bottom. A puzzled look appeared on the Captain's face, but there was little he could do, as the coffin had gone straight to the bottom. Maybe weighed down a little too much. Anastasia had found her resting place in an ocean she had traveled so many times.

Wet Paint

Days at sea, I am convinced, are the best part of a cruise. The relaxing in the sun at the ship's pools, the late mornings, a leisurely breakfast with no pressure to go ashore, is what cruising is all about. This is true for the passengers as well as the crew. Of course, we all go on a cruise or to sea, to see something of the world, and at first a great number of places appear very attractive. Of course a cruise without ports would be pointless. After all, everybody wants to go somewhere. Wouldn't it be odd to report to your neighbor, during the weekly Tuesday evening of bridge, that you didn't go anywhere, only to sea, and that too for two weeks! Gossip about you would run wild and friends would start avoiding you, putting your mental stability in question. It is a fact however, that the more experienced a cruiser becomes, the more he or she appreciates the sea days. Those who ponder making their first cruise, often go for the itinerary, crammed with as many ports as possible. To me it seems that we are not doing that great a job in informing our prospective passengers by bringing the sea days to their attention in all their glory.

While it's not unusual that a brochure allocates half a page describing the joys and pleasures of each port of call, the sea day is mostly simply called 'Sea Day'. Experienced cruisers often read between the lines of those brochures and look for what is not there.

It was one of those sea days, a most beautiful one in the Caribbean, the sun was shining, not a cloud in the sky and a light wind kept the temperature to a level, that was just right.

The previous day we had sailed from Curacao and were en route to Barbados just about half way into our ten day cruise. I was on duty on the bridge for the 12 to 4 watch and in the best of possible moods. Outside, on each bridge wing, crewmembers were hard at work, keeping me company. On one side, a sailor was sanding and varnishing the teakwood railings to a dark and rich tint. A job, which even by simply watching it gave me huge satisfaction. Wood is such a beautiful material and applying the varnish, making it gleam like a mirror, while at the same time being outside certainly is not a job to complain about. Every now and then I walked outside and chatted with the sailor painting, and he explained to me how he did his job.

"Varnishing is more difficult than you think, sir. First you have to use rough sand-paper, then give it a coat of varnish. Then you do it with a finer grade and give it another coat."

"What's in there?"

I pointed at an unmarked can containing a watery substance.

"Oh, that's the converter sir, you add it and then the varnish dries faster. The more you add, the faster it dries, feel it."

I made a mental note to remember this, as I was planning to pursue an advertisement I had seen, announcing a little wooden sailing boat for sale, which without question would need tons of varnish.

"Feel it, I only did this part half an hour ago and it's almost dry."

The man was right. It was amazing. The railing shone like a mirror, and he only just had finished working on it.

"Oops, almost three, time for coffee."

The sailor put his brush in a can with thinner, closed the can with varnish, and with a 'See you later,' he went down to the mess room. I too went inside and poured myself a cup.

Sipping on it, while leaning on the windowsill, looking out over the blue sea, I was at peace with the world.

Now, that I have at length mentioned the sailor painting, you might want to know what crewmember was so hard at work on the bridge wing at starboard side. Well, at that side there was the captain, working very hard to get a nice suntan. He had organized a deck chair with a little table, and with the bridge wing being a restricted area, he was alone, and had all the privacy he could wish for.

I only had been on board for three weeks and it was the first time I had ever sailed with him. Already, during a few occasions, I had found out that he was not exactly an easygoing man. It still upset me thinking back on how he had reprimanded me in public for only the smallest offence. Therefore, I had stayed away from the starboard wing.

Every now and then I peered out of the side window and saw that his many days of hard work were paying of. His whole body was tanned a deep color of brown. It even could be seen underneath the thick lavishly curling hair on his barrel shaped chest. The man must be strong as an ox, I reflected. While fairly short, he could not have been much taller than 5 feet 6, and looked to be almost as wide as that.

Turning back, I took another sip of my coffee, watching the far horizon. Far away, I saw some movement. I put the cup down. Did I see a whale spouting in the distance? Reaching for my binoculars, I stepped back a few paces. Yes I was right, a few miles ahead of us I saw a group of whales, maybe six or seven. Even though seeing those great mammals is not that exceptional, observing a whole group is not a daily, or even a monthly occurrence. Should I make an announcement? The passengers without doubt would love to see this.

Using the public address system though, put me in a quandary, as this was discouraged by our company. The passengers were supposed to be on board to relax, not to listen to all kinds of announcements. But surely, a group of whales would be of enough interest to warrant this disturbance? Not wanting to receive another dressing down, for a moment I stood in quandary. Suddenly a brilliant idea popped up in my mind, why not ask the captain? He was close by and his agreement would cover any comments I could get.

"Sir, there are whales close by, should I make an announcement for the passengers"?

"Huh, what?....Whales? Where? Yes of course, they will love it, where do you see them?"

"At the other side, about a mile away now, must be about seven of them."

Apparently very interested in marine life, the captain got up, grabbed a pair of binoculars from the bridge and hurried to the other side, while I made the announcement.

"Ladies and gentleman, we are approaching a group of whales on our port side..."

My announcement must have been heard by every soul on board, and within a few minutes the railings were lined with hundreds of passengers and crew alike. So many were there, that the ship slightly listed under their combined weight. The captain was no less enthusiastic than anybody else.

"Look there, he must be at least a hundred feet, and that one, look!"

It was obvious that I had misjudged this man slightly, as someone who had such an obvious love for nature around him and could show so much appreciation for these magnificent creatures, could not be too bad a human being either. After we had passed the whales, a short while later, I went back inside, after all, an officer on duty should not stay outside and away from his instruments too long.

After a while however, it did puzzle me that the captain

remained outside, still leaning heavily on the railing looking at something far away.

"Hhggnnnaagggnn…!" I nearly dropped the binoculars I had just picked up to see for myself what the captain, outside, was still looking at. What a horrible sound. Had we hit a whale or what? Quickly I opened the door to the bridge wing.

"Did you hear that? What was it?"

The captain still had his back turned to me when he answered, his voice sounding uncommonly muddled.

"Get me off, I'm stuck to the railing!"

"You're what?"

"You idiot, can't you see that I'm stuck, couldn't you come out when you saw that the whales had left."

"But what…, what do you mean?"

"I'm stuck to the varnish! Don't you get it, you block-head? And don't talk so loud, before you know it the passengers will see me."

I must say that at first I did not know what to do. The captain, except from making grunting sounds, trying to get off, didn't offer any solutions either, so it took me a while to get my wits together. Call for help, that would be the best, after all, I could not leave the bridge.

"He is stuck to the what?"

The staff captain, woken from his afternoon nap, had to be told two times before he began to understand the situation even remotely, and one more time to convince him that his navigator was not affected by a severe case of sun stroke. A few minutes later, still tucking his shirt in his pants, he was on the bridge and together we walked outside where the Captain still stood, making valiant efforts in pretending that he was watching the horizon.

"Hello sir. Are you stuck?"

A strangled sound came before the poor man answered.

"Yes, you nitwit, what do think, I'm stuck to the wet varnish."

The staff carefully touched the railing next to the captain. "It's dry now." He uttered stupidly

"Yes, I know, but it was not earlier, I leaned on it when he called me for those stupid whales."

As it turned out, I was not the only one having difficulties finding a solution. Like me, it also took our staff captain a while to get his thoughts together, as clearly he was as much at a loss as I had been earlier. To be honest, it was a bonus for both of us that the poor captain was stuck with his back to us with little chance of him suddenly turning around, as what he would have seen then would certainly have caused a few dismissals. Both of us, at last, clearly saw the whole situation in its true context and we had a very hard time not to laugh out loud. The poor staff captain was red as a beet and I saw him closing his eyes when he spoke again, tears rolling down his cheeks.

"Let me get you off sir, one moment."

Without warning he grabbed the distressed and unsuspecting captain by his shoulders and vigorously pulled him back as hard as he could.

"AAAAUUUUWWWW, you idiot, what are you doing, butcher, you ...."

The captain, it was clear was quickly loosing what little patience he had left, and kept going for a while, describing in very explicit terms of what he thought of his staff captain and what he would do, once he would get off the railing. This, to us of course, in no way was an incentive to get things going.

"You really are stuck."

The staff captain observed, after having looked at the situation in front of him.

"Your armpits too. Let me get the carpenter."

After that, it didn't take very long before the bridge was a scene of frantic activity. Every officer suddenly had some urgent business, that required him to be there, and of course have a peek outside at where two carpenters were busy working around the Captain to unscrew the wooden railing part from the steel stanchions. When it finally came loose, between the two of them, they carried the piece of teakwood inside, the captain still stuck to it, struggling in the middle. Once inside we carefully put a chair behind him, while one end of the railing was put to rest on the maneuvering console and the other on a bookcase.

"Get out of here, all of you."

He hissed to the assembly of onlookers, with such venom in his voice, that it took less than a minute for everybody to disappear. Except of course for the carpenters, the staff captain and me. Never before did I have such an eventful watch with so much excitement on the otherwise so quiet bridge.

Slowly, hair-by-hair, the captain was cut loose by the carpenter. It took almost two hours in which I learned how creatively a person under extreme duress could use his language and I was impressed. The captain also gained my grudging admiration for not having a massive heart attack during the whole embarrassing episode. Finally the job was finished and within seconds he disappeared, his arm held high, as not to touch his tender parts and a bright red beam of bare skin on his chest, which looked as if a farmer had passed to cut the grass.

It's a strange thing maybe, but I never bought myself the wooden sailing boat I always had wanted so much.

The Falkland Islands

The Falklands, or the Malvinas, as they are known in Spanish speaking countries, is not a place frequently visited by cruise ships, or any ship at all for that matter. It is a far off windblown place a great distance off the coast of Argentina in the South Atlantic. In all my years at sea, I have visited the islands only once, a visit never to be forgotten. Our call at Port Stanley, started normal enough, a little windy maybe, but otherwise a perfect day, cool and crisp, or so it seemed.

Standing on the bridge wing that morning, looking down at the guests disembarking into the waiting tenders, I could hardly wait till the end of my shift to join them. A call at the Falklands in our industry is so rare, that I wanted to make the most of it, and spend as much time ashore as I could.

If I had known that I would get far more than my share of the island I was so looking forward to exploring, my eagerness would certainly have changed into hesitance. Normally, when handing over my duties to a colleague, I take my time with it. We have a coffee together and chat about whatever is on our minds. Not this time, however. Less than five minutes after he had appeared on the bridge, I was boarding one of the boats to bring me ashore.

Luckily, from being out on the bridge wing that morning, I knew that it was rather cool outside, and I was dressed in my old uniform bomber jacket. The ride to the island took about 20 minutes as the ship was anchored in the outer sound. At first I hardly noticed that the wind was picking up, pre-occupied as I was with my surroundings. After we arrived at the dock I felt a cold wind gusting up, creating white caps in the harbor. I shivered in my warm jacket and pulled the zipper up even higher.

Being rather inexperienced in weather changes in these parts and maybe not putting one and one together, I decided to walk into the town to see what there was to do and look at the sights. It didn't take me long to discover that Port Stanley, the Capital of the Falkland Islands, as a town, will never be a hot spot for tourists, as there was nothing to do and little to see.

This, by no means meant that I didn't enjoy my visit immensely. The harbor counted numerous ship wrecks, most of them leftovers from another time. Once proud sailing ships, they had limped into Port Stanley and were abandoned by their crew after a wrecking passage around Cape Horn. Being a ship lover, I stood there for a long time, gazing at them, contemplating the fate of those ships and that of their crews. Such gracious lines, so elegant and so much more beautiful, even in their derelict state, than any modern day ship.

I shivered again, and looked around for a place of shelter, as the temperature seemed to have dropped to below freezing levels. Suddenly my spirits rose. 'Harry's Bar', a signboard proclaimed. It was nailed un-expertly to a wall of a small tattered building at the opposite side of the street. I was cold to the bone and certainly a little snifter would do rather nicely. In my eyes, the place seemed to be a safe bet, in that I would be able to do so anonymously. Certainly it was not a place our passengers, being used to the best in life, would visit. It was a likely location to meet some of the local population.

I stopped in the entrance and looked around. It was exactly as expected. A half dark room with some well used wooden furniture, a red-hot stove at the center of it, radiating a warmth which at once made me feel comfortable, even welcome. Stepping forward, I noticed a few bearded guys sitting in a corner, playing a card game. Each had a small glass in front of him. A shiver went up my spine again. I was really cold and the contents of those glasses looked very appealing.

"One, the same please."

I said to a small woman behind the bar.

"You're with the army?"

It was more a statement than a question. At first I could not figure out why the bearded man, who had turned around to me, thought I was with the army. But then I realized why. The war had only ended a year before, and every stranger in the little town must be 'army' in the local people's eyes. Before I could explain, he started talking again.

"I'm here for the army as well, didn't expect that eh?"

Not explaining to him that in my thoughts I automatically assumed he was a local. I must confess that putting him in the army would never have entered my thinking. He had a long curly beard, a sweater, which looked like a hand me down of many generations and high leather boots, which never in their life had received a proper polish. No, he could be anything but army.

"I'm with the Irishman."

He exclaimed proudly. I always appreciate it when people are proud of their company and their country and turned to his tablemate.

"So you are from Ireland."

He looked at me, puzzlement showing in his deep blue eyes.

"From Ireland? Me, no, what makes you think so?"

"Well, I thought your friend said..."

The bearded man, looked at me, disgust clearly showing. For a few moments he seemed to be struggling between either turning away from me and resuming his card game or carrying on with his desire to explain. He snorted.

"No man! The tugboat, 'Irishman'. Didn't you see that big ocean going tug when you were in town. Man you must be blind. She is the biggest ship in port."

I didn't want to tell him that my interest this day was more involved with the old sailing ships than with a tug boat, ocean going or not. Probably worse in his eyes, and not mentioned by me, was the fact that I had completely overlooked his pride. Elaborating on our giant cruise ship, which was at least 50 times bigger than his craft didn't seem wise to me either. I nodded yes, and confirmed that I had seen his ship.

"I'm with a cruise ship, we arrived this morning."

"You shouldn't have come in today, those cruise ship guys don't know anything."

With another snort he had turned away from me, directing the second half of his sentence to his tablemate. His remark however, spurred my curiosity.

"What do you mean, that we should not have come in?"

He turned around again, and patiently, as if talking to a small child, he explained. "Can't you read the weather? It's going to be nasty today."

"But we checked the forecast, and it was not bad at all."

"Ha, well if you listen to those weather boys, you will never get it right. No, look at the sky, listen to the weather, sniff it, feel your corn. Mine are aching like crazy. Yes sir, it's going to blow."

"Your 'corn'? You mean those things on a toe?"

I asked dubiously. Of course, over time, I had heard the stories about old seamen, predicting dramatic weather changes and making decisions based on aching toe corns. I had never actually met somebody belonging to that old breed.

"Look outside, look at the weather." He reiterated.

Turning to the window, I had to admit, that even without a corn, the heavy rollers on the harbor, boded little good. Even in the short time I had spent in the bar, the weather had badly deteriorated. I decided to go back the tender landing and see if everything was going well on board. Maybe I was needed.

Once outside again, I had to lean into the wind to fight my way back. A long line of passengers I saw from a distance fore-warned me of trouble, and I increased my pace against the ever stronger wind. The scene I found was one of chaos. One of the Security Officers stood at the tip of the pier, trying to do all kinds of things at the same time, while being beleaguered by at least 25 men and women who wanted to know what was happening. Two sailors were bailing water out of a tender, while the other three tenders were sheltered from the heavy seas behind one of the old shipwrecks.

"What happened, why is the line so long, can't you get them back to the ship?"

"Am I glad to see you!"

Relief showed on his face. At last he could share the wrath of the irate passengers with someone else.

"This last tender came back, couldn't make it to the ship in those heavy seas. The ship appears to be in trouble. The anchor is dragging and they are trying to make steam to get out."

Quickly I tried to assess the situation. A line of at least 300 elderly passengers, tried in vain to find shelter behind an old warehouse. Meanwhile our boats, although safe, were unable to get them back to the ship, and the weather was getting worse by the minute.

"I lost radio contact with the ship twenty minutes ago. The batteries of Walkie-Talky gave out and nobody can come ashore anymore to bring new ones." The Security Officer wailed.

It took a moment for me to take it all in. The ship in trouble, and me ashore, what to do now? Suddenly I grabbed in the back pocket of my jacket. A stroke of good luck! Earlier that afternoon, when on my way ashore, while sitting down in the tender I had discovered that I had forgotten to leave my radio onboard. It was sitting in one of the many pockets of my jacket, together with a spare battery. Forgetfulness turned into a blessing. I switched it on and called the ship.

"We are trying to get out of here."

The Captain told me. The strain in his voice clearly showed how tense he was. "We are sitting in a tight spot, close to the rocks and I need to turn the ship into the wind to get out, but with this storm blowing it's impossible."

In the distance, behind a few little rocky islands in the bay, I could see the funnels of our ship spewing out heavy black smoke. Proof that the engineers were doing their utmost, to help the Captain out. It was a dangerous spot indeed that they were in, and to me, an onlooker from a great distance, it was no at all clear how the Captain would be able to get her out.

I stood there watching the ship and holding the radio so tight that my knuckles turned white. Suddenly an idea flashed through my brain, I pushed the 'send' button.

"Hang on there, I'll send you the 'Irishman'."

"What, who? What Irishman?"

I had already turned around and as fast as I could, was running back to the little bar. This time, with the wind in my back. It was so strong that I was not able to stop myself until I had passed Harry's bar by at least 50 yards. Out of breath and struggling to close the door against the wind, I yelled to the bearded fellow.

"Get that tug of yours going, our ship is in trouble. She is almost on the lee shore. Hurry, you have to push her bow around so she can get out!"

Whatever my earlier thoughts about this man were, I have

to take it back. His reaction was instantaneous and impressive. This of course fueled by the smell of salvage money and a hunter's instinct, which is dormant in every tugboat skipper. It didn't take him more than one second to get going. The move that he made could not be bettered by any professional actor, not even after many hours of rehearsing. While emptying his glass in a smooth move, with one hand, with the other he grabbed in his pocket and produced a radio as well. The moment he brought the radio to his mouth, a stream of orders started cascading from his mouth.

"Gerry, there's an urgent job, get the engines started, blow the whistle to alert anybody ashore, get the towlines ready, tell John, to start casting off the lines. I'll be on board in two minutes."

During that short conversation, he even managed to put on his jacket, and reach the door.

"Tell them to hang on, we'll be there in 20 minutes, 8000 horsepower."

He yelled at me, while running at full speed against the wind. I could not keep up at all as I stumbled behind him. He increased the distance between us every second, and the by now, hurricane force winds, which slowed me down to an almost standstill, did not seem to have much effect on him at all. Before I even reached the dock where the tug was moored, I saw a heavy plume of smoke erupting from the funnel, indicating her main engines were being started. Her crew was already releasing her mooring lines as well.

The reaction of our Captain, when I told him that help was underway, was one of immense relief. It didn't take very long before I saw our ship slowly turning into the right heading towards the ocean. The tug dwarfed by the size of the enormous cruise ship, seemed like a little David attacking Goliath. Again, similar to what was told in that well known old story,

David was the hero.

From the radio traffic I could hear that they were heaving in their anchors, and less than half an hour later, I saw the ship building up speed, and heading out to sea. The Irishman came back to her berth. Her Skipper was on the bridge chewing tobacco had a big smile on his face. Everybody started cheering him, including me...

Then, suddenly reality struck. Our ship had left without me, and not only me, at least 300 of our elderly guests were standing on the pier with me. All of us must have come to the same conclusion simultaneously and we also realized how cold we were. I called the ship on the radio.

"Hey, what about us, we are stuck on the pier, when are you coming back?"

The Captain answered me, all stress gone from his voice.

"We can't come back anytime soon, there is a hurricane blowing out here, we are in for a terrible night. If we can't get our passengers to the ship soon, you will have to put them in a hotel or so, to spend the night."

"But, I haven't seen any hotels."

With a hollow feeling in my stomach, I turned around and looked at the town of Port Stanley behind me. I could not imagine any hotel in that place, and even if there were one, it certainly would not have more rooms than an average Bed and Breakfast.

I was stuck on the Falklands Islands, with more than 300 passengers looking at me for the solution.

Falkland Islands II

Standing there that afternoon on that pier in Port Stanley, it took me more than a few moments to collect my wits, to say the least. For a little while, I almost panicked. How in the world could I get the passengers back to our ship in this weather? Using the ship's tenders was out of the question. They were sitting behind an old shipwreck, protected from the weather for now. Earlier that afternoon, with the seas not even half as high as they were at present, the sailors already had a hard time keeping them afloat. Going by some remarks I heard on my radio, I understood, that it would be extremely unsafe to go out in a small open boat.

What I needed was local help, and wildly I looked around for ideas of what to do. Help, however was closer than I expected, at least some sort of help. It appeared in the form of my bearded friend, the tugboat skipper. When in a tight spot, it is amazing how fast one can warm up to a complete stranger. Especially if that stranger carries with him even the shortest straw of possible help one can cling to.

"Want a drink?"

He had approached me after mooring his tug, and obviously in a good mood about the unexpected financial bonus this afternoon had brought him, he produced a small flat bottle. Before I even could say yes, one of our passengers, an elderly gentleman who just 'happened' to be standing nearby, took him up on the offer. After going from passenger to passenger, the bottle was empty in less than two minutes. An equally elderly lady handed it back to him.

"Thank you sir, that was very kind of you."

He looked at the bottle and then at the lady and me. His mouth slowly opened as if he wanted to say something. Words, however, did not come. Suddenly I had a brainwave.

"Hey, can I hire your tug? You can ferry them back to our ship! Surely the heavy sea won't affect you too much."

"Huh, what?"

His voice betrayed utter amazement. His empty bottle suddenly forgotten, he looked at me. Disgust and incredulity were fighting for preference in his facial expressions. Then he seemed to burst.

"What do you think I am? Do I look like some sort of ferryman! My ship is a tug Sir! An ocean going tug! No way."

He turned away from me, mumbling very abrasive tugboat skipper's words under his breath. It almost sounded like some faraway avalanche.

"My tug, a ferryboat, what in the world does he think, never in my life...."

"I offer you twenty-five dollars a head."

Though nobody had given me the authorization to do such a thing, I was truly desperate for his help. My desperation most certainly was enhanced by the circle of passengers around me, who showed to be in no mood to deal with an indecisive officer.

The grumbling suddenly stopped. He turned around.

"Twenty-five dollars you said?"

I saw his eyes quickly glancing around him, and I could see that he was making a quick calculation of how much he could make. Without a further thought or the blinking of an eye, he threw his principles overboard.

"I'll have to make two trips, can't carry more than 150 people or so. I'll be pushing it past the limit if I take more than that."

I marveled at him. Just as quickly as he had sprung into action earlier that afternoon, he now accurately calculated the amount of people his ship could safely carry. In the mean time, the rows of our assembled passengers were quickly transforming from self-assured, confident very well to do people doing a world cruise, to a group of shivering and hungry individuals. They all looked at the security officer and me.

"When will you let the tenders go? I'm very cold you know, could catch pneumonia," One growled.

"I left my medicine on board. It's way past the time I should take it." Another wailed.

"I really have to use the rest-room." A lady told me, her face in despair and she had her knees tightly crossed.

Faced with all of this and very likely more to come, I made an instant decision to go ahead and put at least half of them on the tugboat. A solution, providing me with two benefits. First, it gave me a much needed confidence boost, and second, it would reduce my problems by half.

"Alright, half of you, follow this gentleman to that big tug over there, he just agreed to bring you to the ship."

For a moment there was a startled silence among the passengers. Everyone turned around to view our newly found means of salvation. I am not sure if this was caused by the prospect of actually boarding a tugboat, which didn't look all that big, in the middle of a howling storm, or my choice of calling the tug boat skipper a gentleman. He clearly did not look or act the part as he started yelling instructions. I, however, had seen another side of him, and at that particular moment had more confidence in him, than in myself, to at least solve part of the crisis.

"What about us?"

An older man apparently had chosen himself as the speaker of the group left behind with me, after the others, with our

Security Officer in the lead, had taken of for the tug.

"Well, we should find some shelter. I'll try to get in touch with the authorities to find out what they can do. Maybe they can ..."

For a few minutes I kept talking, just to hide the fact that I didn't have the slightest idea of what action to take. Then my words trailed off, as my eyes were focusing on a building across the street. A church! A more fitting shelter was hardly possible.

"You all go over to that church. It should be open. After you're all in, I'll have to figure out what to do afterward."

The black clad figure in the back of the church almost dropped the broom he held in his hands, when suddenly a group of brightly dressed people invaded his sanctuary.

"Where is the ladies room?"

A wind swept blond lady who almost ran him off his feet whimpered.

"Hurry man, I can't hold it much longer."

He opened his mouth, but before he could say anything, the lady swept by him, assuming that the direction he indicated with his broom was the right one.

"Is there only one ladies room here? It's cold. Can't you turn up the heating a little?"

As the church filled up, the astonished custodian found himself answering questions as to why the cistern in the toilet filled up so slowly and telling people not to get onto the pulpit, no matter how cute it looked. The poor man desperately looked in my direction, but didn't get much help. I decided to go outside again. The passengers were inside and safe, at least for the time being. I needed to be alone for a few minutes to figure out what to do next and where to get help. There wasn't much time, as it already was getting dark.

The police could possibly assist us, but where to find

them? I decided to stop a passing car. It was an old Land Rover, seemingly the brand of choice on the island, as I hadn't seen any other types so far.

To ask a question, I poked my head into the open drivers side window and immediately pulled it out again, painfully bumping the back of my head against the upper rim. For a moment I thought I had lost my faculties. Then I looked again, this time staying a bit more clear of the window. Yes, I was right after all, the driver's side was taken by a sheep.

"What do you want?" A cranky old voice said, startling me even more.

"Muuuuuhh," the sheep said.

Shaking off my consternation, it suddenly it dawned on me. This was an English island. The driver was sitting on the other side. Carrying sheep in a front seat might not be a common practice where I came from, but here, those creatures being the mainstay of the economy, it was probably a perfectly normal thing to do. Relieved, I stepped closer again and saw that also the rear of the Land Rover was full of sheep. There were at least ten of them.

"Is there a police station anywhere near, or maybe a hotel? I need help for a group of passengers from a cruise ship."

"Yeah, a police station is here alright, but it's a mile down the road. Get in I'll drive you over."

Get in, between all those sheep? The car looked awfully cramped, even without me. The old man already was pushing the sheep, which I erroneously had taken for the driver, to the back and leaned over opening the door. The smell and the cleanliness inside were not exactly inviting, but I had little choice given the circumstances. After all, beggars never can be choosers. Without further ado, I hopped in the half dark car and sat down. Immediately I felt that something was not right and that maybe I should have walked after all. It was a feeling,

I never expected to remember, a feeling from my very early days. I was sitting in something wet and soft. But alas, with a gnashing of its ancient gears, the car had gathered speed already and this was not a time to be squeamish.

The police officer looked at me as if I had just landed from another planet. His eyes bulged, when being told about what was happening outside his warm little refuge, which made him vaguely resembling the sheep in the back of the car.

"300 elderly people, and you want to put them up in a hotel? But we don't have a hotel here, only a few guesthouses. There's Mrs. Barnes who lets her two rooms and then there's old Jock, but he is sick and..."

His voice trailed off, as he tried to remember who else had rooms available.

"Well, can't you call your colleagues and call the local population for rooms?"

"Colleagues? I'm the only one here. No sir, I wouldn't know what to do."

Suddenly, above the howling wind, I could faintly hear the heavy blast of a ship's horn. Relieved, I turned around, going for the door.

"I don't need help anymore, that must be the 'Irishman' returning. They can take the other passengers to the ship now. Thank you anyway."

Leaving the policeman behind me, I struggled to get back to the harbor. It took me almost an hour against the wind. Reaching the dock, my relief turned into consternation. Instead of an empty ship ready to take a new load, I saw passengers disembarking from the tug. Feeling slightly hopeless, I reduced my run to a walk.

Turning a corner, I found our passengers. They had huddled together again, sheltering from the cold wind, behind the same shed they had used earlier that afternoon. Apparently it had not dawned on them yet that the other half of their group had found comfortable shelter in the church nearby. They were all white faced and horror showed in their eyes. When they saw me, almost to a man, they started yelling at me.

"You put us on that boat. It was horrible, never even saw our ship. We were thrown around and thrown back and forth for two hours. It's all your fault."

I pushed on toward the tug and saw the Skipper. He too looked slightly upset.

"What happened? Why didn't you get them to the ship? Now they are all upset at me."

"Don't blame me!" He yelled back at me.

"Half way, I received a distress call from a fishing boat and had to get there to assist. Took me an hour to get them to safety. By then it was pitch dark and I couldn't go on. Look what they did to my ship and me!"

In the dark, and being in a hurry, I had not paid much attention to his appearance, it being slightly below acceptable standards anyway. Now I did, and stepped back aghast.

"Man, look at you. What happened?"

"Two of them got sick all over me."

His earlier strong voice had turned into a whine.

"All over my ship too, every room and the corridors, it will take days to clean."

I didn't want to be impolite to him, but I had more important things on my mind than the cleaning of a tugboat. I brusquely turned away from him. What to do now? I was back at square one. These people couldn't stay in the church overnight! They needed food and water and some comfort. After all, the majority of them were well into their seventies or beyond. It is well known that during times of crisis the best ideas are born. This time it was no exception.

"All of you get over into the church. I will be back soon."

Again I found myself running with the wind, and this time, through earlier experience, managed to stop my wild run right in front of the door to the police. My sudden idea was spurned by the fact that the war had ended only less than a year before. Surely, there must be a garrison of some sorts where I could ask for help. The police officer was still sitting where I had left them, stirring a cup of tea.

"Call the army commander at the base, I need him now."

"The army commander?"

"Yes, isn't there a base over here? There must be."

After a little more explaining he dialed a number on an old fashioned black telephone and within a few minutes I found myself talking to a colonel. Never before in my life did that cultured British accent please me more than that evening. Quickly I explained what had happened and what I needed. He was my last resort. Hot food and beds I told him and above all medicine for about half my flock. This last request proved to be a problem, as much of what I needed was unavailable on the island.

"Well, old chap, it seems that we have to send a 'chopper' to your ship to pick it all up. I'll send some troop carriers over to start picking them up at the church. In the mean time, from your side you could also start arranging some transport as well, to get them to the base. It's about seven miles you know."

Getting all our guests to the British Army base, proved to be an exercise in its own. Every car I stopped seemed to be afflicted with the same problem. They all had seen heavy use, carrying sheep very regularly, without benefiting from any cleaning effort between the jobs. Motivating elderly ladies, used to being chauffeured in Rolls-Royces, to climb into a Saracen troop carrier wasn't easy either. It took us more than two hours, before the last passengers had vacated the church, leaving behind a bewildered vicar, and a hopelessly stuck toilet system.

The army base was not at all what I expected. It turned out to be a big floating barge, with a sort of containerized building on top of it, three levels high. Soldiers were busy carrying their belongings out to camp in the open, while passengers were ushered into the small cubicles, which, with four to a room looked impossibly small to me. On the first floor, was a big cafeteria, where I found most of our passengers. They were noisily slurping from cups filled with a greasy, but scalding hot soup, hurriedly thrown together by a big jolly army cook.

I smiled, when I saw Mrs. Fox happily slobbering the soup down and chewing on a piece of stale bread. Only the previous evening, she had loudly and in public read me the riot act during our formal dinner. Stating that the caviar she was served was of a quality below any standard she was used to, and expected. Only Caspian Caviar was good enough she had stated loudly. Strange, how quickly circumstances can reduce us human beings to first satisfying basic needs.

I didn't get much sleep that night, and spent most of it checking the weather and staying in touch with the ship. She was 50 miles away, well clear of any land, fighting the gale. The next morning, the wind seemed to die down a bit and I asked the Base Commander for some men to drive down to the town with me and check on the tenders in order to get them started.

"Wouldn't waste too much time son, the weather is very unpredictable. This lull will not last very long. Better call your Captain to come in to get your behinds out of here fast, before the next gale blows in."

I agreed, having had my fill of the Falkland Islands, I was looking forward to a warm shower and, certainly after my ride in the Land Rover, a change of clothes. After we heard from the ship, that they could be at Port Stanley within an hour, we suddenly were in a hurry, with most of our guests still asleep. Without much ceremony, but with great effect, our Colonel proceeded to catch the attention of our normally thoroughly pampered passengers by pushing a button. It activated a siren, which would not have been out of place on a warship going to battle stations.

"Yes, son, that's how we do it in the army."

Colonel Keyes really seemed to enjoy himself, and I could have sworn he regretted the fact that we would not stay any longer. I can only say good things about this man and his soldiers. Because of us, they had to stay the night outside in quickly erected uncomfortable tents. With remarkable efficiency, our guests were supplied with a sandwich to go and again ushered in a collection of army transports. Jeeps, Saracens and half tracks, and of course the motley troop of Land Rovers, driven by some of the local population.

Loading the tenders with more than three hundred people, turned out not as easy as expected. Each of the four was designed to hold no more than 45 occupants, and that was pushing it. Also, the army engineers had succeeded in getting the engines running in only two of the four available. The others could not be started and needed towing. It all took a little less than an hour before we arrived safely at our ship, which had come back into the bay. We were received with cheers from all on board, passengers and crew alike. Soon we were on underway to transit the Straits of Magellan.

The Falklands, I have not visited again, but I will never forget my overnight stay there.

Merry Christmas

'Christmas', the word alone creates a feeling of being away from everyday life, away from reality, a feeling of a mystic world, and of warmth. Much more so than ashore, Christmas on the ocean has something so special, so different, that I would not mind celebrating it on board a ship together with my wife every year.

On a ship, so many nationalities participate that it truly can be seen as a celebration of all mankind. Is that not what Christmas is all about? From the East, the West, the North and the South, every race the Earth produces, all together on a ship during the happiest time of the year. The fraternity of the sea gathered for various reasons. The crew is on board to make a living, many of them aching to be with their families. Many of the passengers are here because it is the only time they have a vacation. Others can't stay home; they are lonely, especially during this time of the year. If one thing unites everybody on board, it's Christmas. The others, of different faiths also tend to get swept along in the mood of goodwill and joy.

The absolute highlight of the celebration is the Christmas Choir, put together by the crew. The company is not involved in it, not in the least. That would be too commercial. How it ever started, I don't know, nobody can tell me. It is generally believed that the first Christmas Choirs on board ships, sang their songs in the dark year of the war, when Christmas, even more so than today, represented hope.

Usually the choir consists of several groups, crew from Europe, the Far East, the West Indies, America and sometimes other places. We all walk into the big lounge, carrying candles and singing our songs. Once everyone has reached his place, either on the stage or in front of it, each group sings in their own language and according to their own culture. This is followed, by a communal singing of internationally known carols like Silent Night.

The result is not so easy to describe, when those hundreds of crew sing together. The Filipino men and women with their beautiful voices, the American entertainment cast using their considerable talent, the West Indians with their natural feeling for music and rhythm and the Europeans...well, in the case of the European officers, they would not be any one's first choice to perform and certainly not to sing! Their voices are better suited to converse next to a running diesel engine or to talk during a hurricane. But even so, the officers sing their songs and do this with a dignity, that is admirable.

Organizing the choirs is by no means a small task and weeks before one can see some nervous activity. Good willed amateurs from each group try to create order in what generally could be described as chaos. Almost always they are successful. Groups rehearse till late at night; they try to agree on what song to sing and who should go in first. After all, who would like to walk into a packed room first, singing and holding a candle? Then, close to Christmas, they all rehearse together once or twice. All this rehearsing is hard work and by far not everybody shows up every time. Work hours, sleep and sometimes the attitude of, "I know the song so why should I rehearse", take their toll. On Christmas Eve however, they show up in great numbers.

I mentioned that almost always it is a success. Only once, as far as I can remember, things went wrong. This was on Christmas Eve, 1984. When talking about it with old friends, who were there, we still have a chuckle and feel embarrassed.

The embarrassment is really not too bad, as I truly believe that most of our passengers did not even notice what really happened.

In all honesty I have to say that what went wrong, was not our fault. The problem started with somebody who should have known better. It was a new idea our cruise director had. During the rehearsals, he did not seem too happy with the program, and he was seen pacing around and muttering to himself. Then on a Wednesday evening he announced what had been bothering him. The choir needed special effects. Special effects for a Christmas choir was something new to us and while we all were curious, we did not realize that we should be apprehensive instead.

While the Americans were singing that they were dreaming of a white Christmas, it really should start snowing, he stood in front of us moving his arms around so vividly, that some of us started to look at the ceiling, expecting the snow any moment. This was not at all a bad idea. The passengers would love it. Through a friend he could get hold of a snow machine. Rick said, It would eject snow when set up. The word 'eject' should have made us wary, but we were not alert and went along with his idea. Also the fact that the machine would come on board a few days before Christmas, effectively limiting the chances of a try out to zero, did not sct of anybody's alarms.

There is a science, that studies how accidents take place. The conclusion usually is that a whole chain of small events can lead to disaster. If ever the Christmas of 1984 on board our ship were investigated, the conclusion would very likely be the same. Lots of small things went wrong, each insignificant. Had we not been lucky as well, our guests would have a show they would remember for life.

The major contributing factor to what went wrong was

that a few weeks before Christmas our purser went on vacation; the one man who was the driving force behind all the organization necessary for the big event. Rehearsals were taken over by his replacement, a small spectacled man who seemed to be carrying the worries of the whole world on his stooped shoulders.

"Christmas is a celebration of joy and we have to try to send this message to our guests."

I can still hear him say, his face showing anxiety, his sad eyes looking at us. The sadness in his eyes seemed to be exaggerated by his glasses, that were of a thickness not often encountered. The few rehearsals went well enough, that is to say for the Filipinos, the West Indians and the Americans. The Europeans were doing well too, at least if I listened to Fred, the purser, who daily reported the progress. From other sources, I must admit, the reports were less flattering.

Christmas Eve came, and the decorations, the trees and the mood of the guests and crew alike had made a wonderful atmosphere invade the ship. Every one was merry and in good spirits. Even Fred managed a smile and succeeded in not looking too unhappy. At ten that evening, we all assembled backstage. That was where the first error became apparent, as far more people showed up than ever during rehearsals. The space filled up till it almost burst with bodies. Fred was sweating. He and a few assistants were handing out menu cards, on which the texts of the various songs were printed. Another thing they handed out were candles, to be held by each, in a holder of aluminum foil. In the dimmed light we would look spectacular, walking in lines from two sides, slowly filling the stage.

Exactly at 10.30 pm we heard the cruise director announcing the choirs to the expectant passengers, and the music started playing. Fred took charge.

"You first, and the others will follow you, come on start singing."

"What me? I can't go first, let somebody else."

A tall robust engineer stood in front of him, trembling with the thought of having to go into the lounge filled with a thousand people, singing.

"Yes you, go now."

"No, please, I can't."

"Oh, alright, I will go first."

Fred realized that somebody had to take the lead, and walked into the lounge. 'Deck the Halls' sung by him sounded more like an ancient ballad, but that was not really what surprised the guests. Back stage, the discussion had erupted who would be second. While this went on, Fred not sensing that everything was not entirely going according to the plan was already halfway across the lounge before he looked back. Nobody had followed him. Needless to say this discovery was quite unsettling. It was at this time that he started to regret using aluminum foil to hold a candle. Hot wax dripped on his hands.

"Aauw"

The discussion behind the stage stopped and seeing Fred's predicament we all walked out, each carefully balancing his candle, all singing along. The audience was impressed. At the head of the column walked Fred, carefully avoiding any further contact with his dripping candle. He reached the steps to the stage and climbed up.

The Europeans were planted on the stage, the Americans in front, and in front of them the West Indians and then the Filipinos. Fred overlooking all the people scrambling on became a little worried. During rehearsals he had never seen so many, and the stage was not that big.

"Move over." He whispered, "More to this side, squeeze

in."

Following his own advise, Fred did a step back.

"Aaah!"

For the second time in a short while, he got the undivided attention of everyone in the room, guests and crew alike. Wildly waving his arms, he tumbled off the stage, right into the Christmas tree. After a few seconds of silence, a roar of laughter erupted from more than a thousand throats and Fred climbed back on stage. Luckily the tree was well fastened and apart from Fred's pride and a dozen crushed dummy presents under the tree, nothing suffered any damage.

The first songs came from the Filipinos, beautifully done and very successful. It was not until the West Indians were singing that I noticed that the shore excursion manager standing next to me, showing less than undivided attention. He started to lean on me very heavily and to my horror I realized that he had had too much to drink.

"What are you doing, why did you show up like this, never even saw you at the rehearsals," I whispered furiously.

He looked at me stupidly.

"I just follo… followed the others."

At that moment the cruise director announced that the following song would come from the officers. The music started and we all started to sing. But not the shore excursion manager, well, he did sing, I have to give him that, but it was completely the wrong song. Worse, it was not even in the menu and had nothing to do with Christmas. It sounded like 'Roll out the barrel'. Others too had noticed the problem, and in a concentrated effort to cover his voice, we all started to sing as loud as possible.

The Christmas Carol must have sounded like a marching song of Atilla the Hun, but we were successful in blocking out Ronald's singing. Suddenly there was some commotion on the other side of him. An engineer, his full attention on singing the carols, had not given too much attention to Ronald's swaying back and forth. He uttered a few heavy words, not at all in line with Christmas and none too soft either. To my consternation I saw that his menu had caught fire when Ronald unwittingly had moved his candle under it. Throwing his menu on the floor the engineer started stamping on it and without too many people actually seeing what was happening he managed to put the fire out.

By this time, most of us were deeply worried about what else would go wrong. I'm sure that some silent prayers went up asking for help. Of course I will never know if God was too busy or simply had too much fun. Our predicament had not ended yet.

With our attention occupied by immediate issues, we had all forgotten about the cruise director. He was behind us, frantically trying to fire up his snow machine. As it was on loan from a friend, of course it had not been necessary to test it beforehand.

Nervously Rick manipulated the buttons. The red light was burning, so what was wrong. He looked into the ejection pipe to see if it was blocked, no nothing at all.

"Whaaam"

The machine had come to life, a solid artificial snowball exploded in his face. The only things he saw, were multicolored stars instead of snow. We never found out what exactly the problem was with the machine. Either the snow was out dated or it just malfunctioned. What happened was that every few seconds a solid snowball erupted from it and came flying over our heads. Of course the balls did not stay in the air, but came down, and as the gun was pointed in one direction, they all came down in the same location. It was our chief electrician, who while singing about a white Christmas   suddenly felt a snowball exploding against the back of his head. Not easily detracted he kept singing at first. But when the snow from repeated hits started to slide down from his head, behind his glasses and into his nostrils, the poor man could not hold out anymore.

"Hatsjee!!"

The violent movement of his body caused the snow to fly around, affecting those near him.

"Hatsjee, hatsjee, hatsjee."

The singing stopped, but the sneezing continued for a while as the snow kept coming. By now the cruise director was trying to stop the machine by shaking it around so vigorously that snowballs were finding their targets left and right, with the same effect they had on the chief electrician. Thank God for the assistant cruise director, who after a short period of paralyzed inactivity, simply pulled the plug. The snowball shower stopped just as fast as it had started. Luckily the more forward situated groups of the choir were not affected and most had not even realized something was amiss.

The singing continued with another song. The majority of the guests had not even seen what was happening thanks to the dimmed lighting. Those who had, most likely had the best Christmas show ever. I know for a fact, that the snow machine is resting peacefully at the bottom of the Caribbean somewhere between Grenada and St. Lucia.

The Lonely Nurse

"Life is beautiful", is the title of a movie that reminds me of life on board cruise ships, more so when talking about the late seventies and early eighties. It was the time when cruising hadn't achieved the status of 'big business' it has nowadays. Even the cruise lines themselves seemed to be quite surprised that their product was appealing to an ever-increasing public and in general seemed slow to take advantage of it.

Maybe because it's so far back now, that the common rule that everything was better then, applies. I for sure do look back at my early years on these ships as the best sailing time in my life. Rules and regulations were less evident and if there were rules, and of course there were, I don't seem to remember them. Sometimes I think it must have been because of coming from the rough and tumble world of cargo ships, that I hardly felt the fact that the discipline had to be fairly strict. Maybe it is because nowadays, I'm the one enforcing them, which makes their presence so much more evident. Not that everything was better though; even though we fondly think back of late nights we enjoyed, we also should guiltily remember the inevitable difficult mornings that followed. These were accepted facts of life it seemed, and I, fresh from cargo ships far more austere, looked at it in amazement.

A third officer feeding the contents of his stomach to the fish when sailing in a lifeboat during a drill, was casually explained to the astonished guests as him being seasick, even though the sea was as flat as a mirror. Such events nowadays could not happen without a one-way ticket being issued to the persons concerned and rightly so.

However, sometimes I wonder, as I can't remember a higher number of incidents in those days. Social life was different too; more officers were seen with the guests in public rooms, interacting with each other and to the benefit of all. Nowadays the workload is such that there is scant time to socialize and sit down for more than half an hour or so. Crewmembers hardly have time for each other and that sadly was better then.

It was during an Alaskan cruise that our Captain, a jolly, rosy cheeked, man, came into the officer's bar and sat down on a stool between me, and an engineer. He appeared to be nervous, played with the bowl of peanuts in front of him and jerked up straight each time the door opened and somebody came in. At first it didn't catch my attention but slowly it dawned on me that he hadn't said a word. It was a very strange thing for a man who normally thrived on being in the company of others.

"Good afternoon, Captain, can I offer you a drink?"

The engineer was ahead of me asking what I should have done before him. Likely he was puzzled by the same question.

"No, thank you. Do I look sick?"

"Pardon, me? No, you look normal."

Clearly the question of the captain unnerved him, and even more so when our commander pulled down his lower eyelid and faced the poor engineer with it.

"Look, what do you see?"

"Nothing, maybe a little red."

"Of course it's red, I've had it pulled down for fifteen minutes in that hospital, they say I might have the flu." He snorted with contempt. "There's nothing wrong with me, I feel fine."

He turned around and ordered a drink, mumbling to himself. The 3rd engineer and me looked at each other and decided not to comment any further. After all a disgruntled captain is best left alone. To myself however, I promised to check it out, especially the medical part, as I had heard that a new redhead nurse had joined the ship a few days before. A decision, I bitterly would come to regret.

Being responsible for the ship's safety equipment, the next day I decided to check out some fire hoses, particularly those sitting in the hospital area. Always a perfect excuse to be anywhere and to enter any space I saw fit. Carrying out my self imposed duties, it didn't take very long before I met the new nurse. Sitting on my knees, checking a nozzle, somebody tapped me on my shoulders.

"Hi, my name is Vivian. Oh my! Do you look pale! I bet you never sit in the sun, you probably need to take some Vitamin C. Come on. I'll give you some."

A little unsure of what to do, I followed her into the infirmary, where she started to rummage through a cabinet filled with all kinds of bottles and boxes. I must say that I liked her immediately, obviously very caring and willing to go the extra step to take care of the crew. She would do well I thought, being like a mother to our sometimes homesick crew. Looking at her, I guessed her to be at least ten years older than me.

"Don't you think we have a darling captain? Oh he is such a dear."

"Uh, oh, well I don't know..."

Although I very much liked sailing with this captain, I never had thought about him as being a darling. Competent and respected were terms that applied more to the man according to me.

"He is fighting a flu, the poor man. He doesn't want to hear about it, but I'll take care of him; I already brought him some goodies."

A few hours after this, I was on the bridge. We were leaving St. Thomas, that most breathtakingly beautiful island, part of the Virgin Islands. The captain seemed to be on edge, as he kept pacing back and forth, his face dark as an approaching thunderstorm.

Seemingly for no particular reason, with a very audible thud, he suddenly slammed his coffee cup onto the windowsill, startling the pilot next to him not a little bit.

"I'm getting fed up with her. Look what she put in my mailbox."

Without further comment he left, and returned a few minutes later with a small shopping bag and held it open in front of the staff captain who had come on the bridge in the mean time and who curiously peered inside. It must be something rather interesting as I saw the Staff's head slowly coming up; his eyes wide open, registering a bewildered disbelief.

"Well, what do you think?"

The captain asked him, his voice more in a tone of command than a question. Unlike me, who slowly started to understand some of the Captain's predicament, apparently the staff captain must have been totally in the dark. He looked at his boss, very much like a doctor who has just diagnosed some disgusting disease for one of his patients.

"Well, what am I supposed to think? I see a bag full of half eaten cookies and some vegetables, I think they are artichokes."

"Right, you are right, they are artichokes."

The poor staff captain clearly understood less and less of the situation, and did a few steps back, while grabbing a pair of heavy binoculars, as if he preparing to fend of an assault by a captain who clearly had gone of his rocker. The captain however seemed to have forgotten about the shopping bag.

"What should I do, she keeps calling me to make sure that I take all kinds of pills. She makes me aware of all kind of diseases I surely will catch; she sends me artichokes because they are rich in some kind of vitamin, the name of which I forgot. Now she wants to talk with me about my future. Probably to tell me that I just contacted some kind of tropical disease."

A wide smile slowly spread across the face of the staff captain. There was no danger here, and possibly a lot of fun instead, at the expense of his boss of all people.

It was obvious that our captain was desperate with the situation and over the course of our departure he and the staff captain discussed what had to be done. As I overheard most of the conversation, I must admit, and guiltily so, that not all the advice the staff captain offered was solid. Even during times when the navigation of the ship needed the captain's attention, I saw him turn away and laugh silently, his hand covering his mouth.

"So you tell me, I should meet her on neutral ground to tell her to stop bothering me, and not in my cabin."

"That's correct, I would meet her in a passenger lounge, after all she can't do a thing there, lots of people around."

"But I don't want to discuss my health, even if she only makes it up. What would the guests think about me having yellow fever or something like it." The conversation lasted another 10 minutes before the captain left. The moment the door closed behind him, the staff captain burst out laughing and didn't stop for fifteen minutes. Between bursts of laughter, interrupted by gasps for breath, he tried telling me exactly what was going to happen.

The nurse had insisted on meeting him, apparently to talk about his health and the Captain, normally so adept at solving any problem he came across, this time was faced with a persistence he was at a loss of how to resist. She was adamant, and it clearly showed in her actions. He, the staff captain had advised him to talk with her in a guest lounge. A cabin or the hospital, he had convinced the captain, were too dangerous.

And he had agreed. Another rasping laugh, indicating the staff's vocal cords were not used to all this exercise.

I failed to understand the real funny part about this public room thing, and expressed my lack of understanding.

"Don't you see, it's a public room, and at eight tonight you and me are going to be there. I wouldn't want to miss this for two months salary."

I started to smile and looked admiringly at him. What a true genius! This was a person one could learn a lesson or two from.

Ten minutes to eight, we walked into the 'Seafarer Lounge' and saw Vivian sitting at a table along the wall, a clipboard in front of her. She couldn't have selected a better location, as her bench seat had an extremely high back while right behind it was a vacant table. It enabled us to sit practically back to back, and hear the whole conversation while enjoying a cool drink.

It took quite a while before the captain arrived and we almost started to think that the staff captain's wise counsel had gone unheeded, when we suddenly heard Vivian loudly cry out.

"Captain, johooo, I'm over here."

We didn't actually see the Captain as he was hidden from us by the high backrest, but we could see most of the guests as they all turned their heads towards the sound. By following the direction in which the passengers looked, we could figure the progress of the captain through the room. The staff captain next to me put his fist in his mouth, and bent over the table, his face bright red with suppressed delight at the obvious discomfort of his superior. As expected, we could follow the conversation word for word.

"Hi Vivian, can I sit down?"

It was clear that the captain tried to steer the conversation away from any medical talk and to our disappointment he was rather successful in doing so. Vivian did not volunteer names of any possible diseases he could have contracted, and even the subject of his lack of sleep, another of Vivian's major concerns, was not broached. To me it appeared that our own position wasn't that great either. We only could sit there, sipping our drinks, as talking to each other, surely would be overheard at the other side of the backrest, and likely our presence would not be very much appreciated by the Captain. Already some of the passengers cast suspicious looks at us, two officers sitting together for almost an hour, hardly saying a word.

"Can I ask you a few questions?"

The staff captain painfully punched me in my ribs. The fun was starting,

"Listen."

Probably because he was lulled into a false sense of security, after all the past hour had been rather pleasant, we heard the captain agree. What followed was a series of questions, which at first seemed innocent enough and we even thought that this too would end uneventful. Whether he liked his job, what he thought of Idaho and whether he had brothers and sisters. Apparently she wrote it all down, as every now and then we heard her asking him to slow down a little. The captain didn't seem to mind, relieved as he must be about the fact that as long as she was writing down innocent and often silly answers, he would get off the hook relatively cheaply.

"How many children do you want?'

Our growing suspicion that the captain wasn't very serious about his answers, proved to be right.

"Oh, let's say about 10 to 12, maybe more."

At that moment, we almost thought that the interview was over, as it took a while before we heard Vivian again. This time her voice sounded strange.

"But that's not possible, that's too many."

"I wouldn't know why not, there are families with more, I once read a book…"

"No, no, your wife is too old, she can't have that many children."

"My wife? But I'm not married, and…"

"No, I mean your future wife, she is too old."

Slowly it must have dawned on our poor commander that a discussion about his health would have been the better option, as we heard him stammering, trying to find words.

"My future wife", but I'm not even dating. I wouldn't know who…"

I almost could picture his face and saw that by now we were not the only ones who showed interest in what was going on. All around the lounge we saw heads turning, some older guests even had their ears cupped with their hands, to miss nothing. This was far more interesting than the trio softly playing music. Music? It had stopped and I noticed the three musicians also had caught onto what was going on in the corner of the lounge.

"Yes, I'm too old to have that many children, three or four are fine with me."

Vivian's voice sounded shrill with emotion. Well she was not the only one whose emotions were badly shaken. The captain's too obviously were badly disturbed. As he answered her, every word, no every letter he brought out was loaded with disbelief and gloom.

" What??? I never said anything in that direction, how in the world could you come up with such ideas?"

There was no answer, at least not in words; instead we heard a long wail followed by sobs and the sound of a falling glass. Then we saw Vivian running across the room and disappearing through the door.

A few minutes later, apparently the time he needed to

gather his thoughts, we saw the captain walking in the same direction. The guests turned away from him in disgust. How could he upset such a nice nurse so much that she had to cry in public? Horrible man, they would write the company about such behavior. I looked at the staff captain and he looked at me. We didn't say anything, but without words we knew that we would keep quiet about this, and certainly about our part in it.

The captain's mood was indescribable for the next few weeks; I never experienced it that bad and it was the staff captain and me who received the brunt of it. Even now many years later, and knowing that Vivian is happily married to a man she caught only weeks after her unsuccessful attempt at hooking our captain, I still feel a little guilty about the whole affair. I know I should not. Our staff captain apparently never felt any remorse. Instead he was the man to marry her.

The Stowaway

Of all the cruises I have ever made, the ones around the world always stand out, and they do so in almost every aspect. Navigation wise, they are the most challenging. The interaction with the passengers is of a far more intense and personal level than on the shorter cruises and the things we get to see are often extraordinary. There is very little routine involved in these voyages. Because of the fact that we visit so many countries, there are very often situations that nobody even remotely anticipates before setting out.

It was towards the end of our cruise around the world and we were sailing in the Pacific Ocean. I was standing on the bridge, a navigation officer, and as such also responsible for all life saving equipment on board. With still a few days to go, on our trip from Japan to Hawaii, I was contemplating everything I had seen and experienced during the last three months.

We had left New York on a cold January day, with ice floating around the ship in the Hudson River. This, I had reflected happily, would be the last ice I would see all winter. It had been cold that year according to the sparse news from home we had received on board. Never having liked real cold weather very much, the situation had suited me perfectly well. I remembered myself, chilled to the bone and shivering, when doing the safety drills and lowering the lifeboats into the icy waters of the river, before setting out on this long voyage. We had to prove our ability to handle every imaginable emergency, to the Coast Guard, before setting out on this cruise; a tedious, but necessary process. I smiled, thinking that the next drill, upon returning to Los Angeles, certainly would be a lot more comfortable. In preparation, I had already started to check all the safety equipment for the third time during that cruise.

Checking my watch, I wondered why my assistant had not returned as yet. Two hours ago, I had sent him out to check the emergency rations in the last four lifeboats and tenders. Surely he should be finished by now. Looking at my watch again, I realized, it was also time to mark the noon position of the ship on the map, as shortly the other officer would arrive to take over my shift. I went over to the map and began my work of plotting the position and calculating the speed.

Then suddenly the peace and quiet was broken. The door to the bridge was slammed open, crashing into the bulkhead with a loud bang. Jumping, I broke the tip of my pencil. Even before I could turn around, my assistant Mark, the Third Officer, came stumbling in, with a wild look on his face.

"Aaaahhhh, man, come over, help, there's a guy.... oh dear...." He mumbled.

"What's wrong, what happened?" I asked.

His face was as white as a sheet and he shook all over his body. It greatly worried me, as something very serious must have happened. Mark, however, was not ready to talk yet. It took us almost ten minutes and two glasses of water, half of which he spilled, to steady him enough so that he could tell us what had happened.

"T..t..there is a bb.. body in the tender."

"A body?... You mean..."

"No, not like that", ...I saw his eyes rolling... "Oh my, I thought I would faint... I opened one of the benches, to check the date on the provisions inside, and there he was, lying on his back, making this gurgling sound..."

I looked around me. My watch relief had just arrived. He, heard only half the story and immediately stated:

"Stowaway, better call the captain."

"Let's check it out first." I said. "Call the bosun and a few sailors to meet us at the tender. You come with me Mark."

The color, that had slowly started to return to his face, drained off again.

"No, please! I am not going back there, you go alone or with the bosun."

Deciding not to argue, I turned and ran. At the tender, the alerted bosun was already waiting for me, ready to ascend the vertical ladder, to get into the craft. As the good man did not know yet what this was all about, he did not protest when I stepped aside to let him go first. I waited till he had been inside for a few minutes, before deciding to follow him. After all, on a vertical ladder, one never wants to be too close behind somebody else, and certainly not now, with the possibility of the bosun backing up in panic.

For a few moments, nothing happened. Then suddenly I saw his face appearing over the railing of the tender. Disapproval clearly sounded in his voice, when he saw that I was still all the way down on deck.

"Come up, quick."

Making an impatient gesture with his hand, he pointed at the ladder. Sensing there was no danger, I spurted up and jumped into the tender. It has been more than fifteen years since this happened, but the scene I encountered in that tender is still vividly with me. There was an open bench, with a skinny human being lying in it, supported by lifejackets and emergency rations. Pathetically, he made feeble attempts to get up, but apparently he lacked the strength to do so. With his emaciated hands he clawed at the rim of the seat. He looked at us with eyes like dark lumps of coal, pleading and filled with immeasurable sorrow. I jumped forward to assist him. A surprisingly easy job, as he barely weighed more than 80 pounds. Noticing the empty cartons around, I concluded that he must have survived on some of the emergency rations in the boat. It took but a few minutes, before we had enough crew together to get him down and in our hospital where the doctors started to work on him. It was not until three days later that our physicians declared him stable and out of danger.

A ship is a small place and news always spreads like wildfire. Some of the passengers, naturally curious, had seen him lowered onto the deck in a stretcher, his hollow face wrapped in blankets. Slowly it dawned on me that while every other person on board the ship had been eating five course dinners, less than a hundred feet away, a fellow human being had been slowly dying of thirst and hunger, afraid to come out of his hiding place into a world of luxury just around the corner.

Then the sentiment amongst our passengers arose, based most likely on their feelings of guilt about having so much. This started a few days later, when the wretched man was brought up to the deck in a wheelchair, to gain his strength and get fresh air.

Everybody wanted to see him, touch him, and feed him, both chicken broth or caviar. One of our passengers, a notoriously selfish man, suddenly saw the errors of his ways and decided that his change should start with our stowaway.

Weren't they on a world cruise?

Wasn't every one of them more than well off?

Shouldn't they help this poor man?

A collection was taken up and everybody gave generously and without reserve. The amount grew and grew till finally there was an amazing sum, big enough to set up any man for a good life.

Our poor stowaway, not even aware of the small fortune amassing behind his back, was pathetically grateful for all the attention he received from the passengers and the crew alike.

Slowly, his story unraveled. He was from Cambodia and had escaped the killing fields with nothing else to show but his life and a broken body. His family was gone. He had wandered around the countryside hiding for months, not even knowing where he was. How exactly he managed to stay alive, we will never know. His body showed the evidence of extensive hardship and he walked with a permanent limp. How he reached the ship was also a mystery. He had hid in a lifeboat for close to a month. Not daring to come out, nibbling on emergency rations his stomach could not handle.

Communicating with him was not the easiest thing. We had been able to find only one crewmember able to understand a few words of his language. Stowaways are never very welcome on any ship. They present the captain with way too many problems. This one created even more sleepless nights, as he did not carry any identification on him and nobody on board could vouch where he came from. The shore side authorities contacted proved not to be too helpful. Most countries have enough refugees as it is and when not sure about their status, usually refuse to admit more. Ships with stowaways on board are even lower priorities. In most cases they are in foreign ports, and officials are often eager to send them off with their trouble. I clearly remember our captain's frustrations, as he took to venting them loudly on the bridge, after each time he had consulted officials ashore.

"Nobody cares. It's not their problem they tell me. I don't know what to do next. If this goes on, he will be on board forever."

I felt for him. Never before had I sailed with a better man. I regretted that he was due for retirement at the end of this voyage. He didn't need all these troubles. In the mean time, our stowaway was slowly becoming the favorite of the passengers and crew, and not without cause. He was polite and friendly to everyone and felt really sorry to saddle anybody with his predicament. This didn't help our captain, of course. Jimmy, he was called by everybody after a few days; his real name was such a tongue twister that after a few tries, everybody had reverted to the so much easier Jimmy, as to the inexperienced ear, it sounded remotely like he pronounced his own name. He diligently tried to make up for the inconvenience he was causing and slowly started to take over virtually every little job the captain had to do, which was not covered by his steward. We all saw this happening. Everybody agreed that this well educated gentleman deserved to receive all the help he could get from us. But then, what could we do?

Our passage through the Panama Canal was uneventful. Finally we were on the last leg of the voyage with only a few more ports to go to. Many of the passengers had already left the ship in Los Angeles and it seemed a little empty with only one half of them left.

One evening, we had the last grand gala party of that voyage, in honor of our Captain's retirement. After a career of more than 40 years at sea, he finally had decided that enough was enough. And what a career it had been! Rising up from the ranks to command one of the most prestigious liners afloat. He was a man hugely respected by all he dealt with. Ever since I had first met him on my second cruise ship, he had been my role model. He represented all of what an excellent captain should be. The reception given for him was truly grand and a long line of passengers, crew and officers lined up to bid him farewell. The most striking thing of all was that to his right, dressed in a three- piece suit, happily shaking all the hands too, was our stowaway.

The next morning our captain came on the bridge with a big smile on his face. I smiled back. Obviously he was reliving yesterday's party, or, was it some good news about our stowaway? I didn't need to probe him to satisfy my curiosity.

"I was getting so fed up with all these evasive answers. Even in our own country, nobody wanted him. Called them again this morning, and again all that bureaucratic talk that he needed papers and you name it."

"But he does not have any papers." I ventured. "We all know that."

"That's what I kept telling them. They didn't even listen when I threatened them and even the Governor."

Our next port of call was one of the Caribbean islands, which as a last remnant of my country's once vast empire, was still strongly connected to the old mother country.

Earlier, I had overheard the captain telling the hotel manager that here was our last chance, in a long time to disembark our unexpected guest. He must have finally gotten through to the Governor, which was no small feat in my eyes.

"You threatened the Governor?" I asked.

"Yes, what do you expect? Nobody will listen otherwise. He didn't care though and laughed at me."

If possible, he rose even higher in my esteem. I could also understand that a governor would not lightly give in to the threats of a cruise ship captain. Worse, there might even be severe repercussions for him. I was worried, but at the same time curious.

The captain still had that big smirk on his face, showing satisfaction instead of defeat. I wondered what possible hold he could have over a governor appointed by the Queen.

Suddenly it struck me...

"You didn't call ...?"

His smile even widened.

"Yes, I didn't know what else to do, so, I called the Queen." He looked at his watch.

"That's twenty minutes ago, so I expect action any moment

now."

I gaped at him. In front of me stood a giant of a man, not so much in stature, but certainly in class! A man, who was not afraid to play hardball, to help others. His prediction proved to be extremely correct. Our Radio Officer, his Adam's apple bopping up and down, ran off again.

"There you are, Sir. The Minister of Foreign Affairs is on the phone. He sounded worried and didn't even mind being put on hold."

"I'll take it here. Just connect him through."

The next few minutes were a delight to my ears. Our captain, in his most authoritarian voice, telling the minister what he wanted done. There were no 'please sirs' or 'sorry sirs' to be heard, at least not from our Captain's side. The conversation had not even ended, when again the Radio Officer appeared again, profusely sweating now.

"It's the Governor sir. He needs to speak with you urgently."

For a moment, the captain cupped the telephone with his hand and turned around saying,

"Put him on hold."

Our radio officer's Adams apple bobbing up and down, he ran off again. It went on for more than two hours, one official after another, calling and assuring the Captain that everything would be done and it would be no problem at all. Our stowaway would receive preferential treatment when applying for a passport. Never before and after, did I witness a more immediate action with help offered by the highest-ranking officials in our country. Our captain had played an ace that nobody knew he held. He had called the 'Boss'.

He enjoyed himself hugely playing with those who had played with him. A few days later he explained to me how all of this was possible. Our Queen and her family had sailed with him often and they had become personal friends. Never before had he even hinted about this connection to anyone.

He left the ship a few days later in New York with the whistles of our ship blowing a farewell in the air, a farewell to one of the last great gentlemen of the sea!

The story of the stowaway lived on. It was repeated and repeated and the stature of this captain rose even more in our eyes.

More than ten years later, now a Captain myself, I was watching television in my cabin. Reporting from somewhere in the world, a CNN newscaster told us about a huge refugee problem in one of the African countries. I watched and my thoughts drifted back in time, to our own refugee Jimmy. Where was he now? What had happened to him? I didn't know. I picked up the remote control, to switch off the television set. The program, in the mean time, had switched to another scene, the United Nations building in New York. The High Commissioner of the United Nations dealing with the refugees was making a speech.

Suddenly I was shocked and my mouth dropped open. I looked again to make sure my eyes were not deceiving me. Sitting behind a delegate desk was Jimmy. Our Jimmy, a little bit older, but nevertheless still the same. He still had those gentle eyes, and that strong chin. He had put on some weight since the time he left the ship in a borrowed suit. From the brass nameplate on his desk, I could deduct that he was one of the personal secretaries of the High Commissioner. My heart raced with excitement! Never could the refugees have had a better advocate. Somebody, who from his own experience, knew what it was like; having to leave one's country, and also, one who knew how it felt to receive kindness.

Pilot on Board

Entering a harbor, without doubt, always is the single most important part of any voyage. Not only does it signal the end of a trip, it also is the most critical part of it. So many things can go wrong while passing through the breakwaters or swinging around in a narrow basin. Currents and wind can combine their strength and push the ship to shallow water, a sudden rain shower can reduce the visibility to zero and increase the wind to a difficult to manage strength. Every captain can be found on the bridge at these times. Usually he appears pretty calm and in control of the situation, at times even cracking a joke. Often though the jokes serve to cover his nervousness. After all, the slightest mistake and the ship could be out of service for months at a time. Not only economic damage for the company and distress for the guests is on his mind; also his own career is on the line, every time again.

Contributing to the captain's anxiety is the fact that although he knows his ship well and feels confident about what he can do with her, often the conditions in a port are very much an unknown factor. What if an engine suddenly fails and he needs tugs, how to call them, how to get help?

Port authorities throughout the world have recognized this fact and have made pilots available to assist him in his task and advise him about local conditions. Not only are pilots available, they even are compulsory to take on board. With a pilot on board with all his knowledge, the worries of a captain are over, one could say. Well, say again. The relationship between a pilot and a captain is a strange one, almost like one

of love and hate. Often one can hear a sigh of relief, the moment
a pilot boards a ship, while at the same time, many captains
seem to have an anxiety attack, fueled by the doubt about the
unknown person invading his domain. Will he be knowledgeable, will he be easy to work with and above all, will he be
able to bring us in safely?

The statement 'I have seen it all' would be very assuming,
but I honestly believe that I have seen most of it. The vast majority of pilots are competent and prudent men. They come on
board and do their job. A small percentage, stand out lonely at
the top, like the few planets, distinctly shining bright amongst
millions of stars. Others, and mercifully there are even fewer of
them, are conspicuous in their inability or incompetence.
Competence or the opposite is not dictated by geographical
location. Often I have heard comments about certain countries,
less developed than others, and automatically assumptions
about the capabilities of pilots were made. Nothing is more
incorrect. Some of the best pilots I have ever worked with, I met
in small far away ports, while the opposite occasionally happens
in some major European, or even United States ports. To be
honest, the complete opposite of course also can be true. Many
a pilot when boarding a ship must have similar feelings about
the Captain and the crew they will have to work with. Captains
also come in all sorts, from stellar performers to mediocre ones.

One of the pilots I have worked with countless times and
whom I most admire is Captain Durward Knowles of Nassau.
Every time when approaching this port I look forward to seeing him aboard. Well into his eighties, he is as sharp and agile
as two others half his age and with his tremendous sense of
humor, he has a natural way of putting everybody at ease. Going
into this harbor through its narrow entrance, rarely is a concern
with him along. There is a book written about his life, called,
'Driven by the Stars' that gives a detailed account of his extraor-

dinary life; his many entries into the Olympic Games, how he won gold there and how he became 'Sir' Durward. However, I often think that a change of the book's title, which refers to the Star Class sailing boats, would be fitting, as with him on board. 'Guided by a Star' would be appropriate.

Sometimes, pilots are on board for an extended time, like in British Columbia and Alaska. Then a good relationship is even more important, as unlike in most ports where a pilot leaves a ship within an hour or so, in this part of the world we work together for the better part of the cruise.

We had left Vancouver and were heading north through Johnson Strait. That part of British Columbia, which is so awesome in its beauty and which to the great loss of the passengers, is almost always passed during the night. I was a senior watch keeping officer and very content doing the dog shift. The pilot who had boarded and I had sailed together many times and spend the dark hours talking about our lives at home and about the darkened land we were passing, when suddenly the door behind us opened and the captain appeared. I immediately felt a little apprehensive and stood up a little more straight, mentally preparing myself for all kinds of questions. There was no reason for him to be up in the middle of the night as the next narrow passage was still over an hour away. Was he checking on me?

"Cooked some meatballs, want one?"

That was a nice surprise and at the right moment too as I did feel a little peckish. Without waiting for an answer the captain put a plate in front of each of us with a steaming hot meatball on it. It was a good thing that he had told me what it was that he had brought, as in the dark it would have been difficult to guess, except of course for the delicious smell. I also saw the pilot dubiously peering at the almost football sized object in front of him.

"Made them myself, my wife's recipe. You like it?"

The smacking sounds in the dark were enough of an answer. I must say that rarely had I tasted such a good meatball and the pilot also commented on this fact after the Captain had left.

"Still had a few left over, thought to bring you one more."

The captain said reappearing again carrying a plate in each hand with a ball of the same size as before. After some hesitation both of us accepted the meatball, which, I must say looked a little less appetizing than the first one. But what navigator, and also what pilot, would dare to refuse such a nice gesture from a captain who obviously is trying to please. Finishing the second plate was difficult and certainly not only for me. Next to me in the dark, I heard some huffs and puffs and finally a sigh of relief when the pilot finished his second plate.

"That was great Captain, never tasted better."

There was no answer as the Captain had left. I looked at the map and saw we were approaching Ripple Shoal, should I call the captain, or should I wait? After all he had just left the bridge, knowing about our position.

"Let's finish them off, just had three left, here you are."

To my consternation, I saw another plate being put in front of me, the contents ominously shining in the moonlight and swimming in gravy. It seemed almost double the size of the earlier ones. Also the pilot appeared to be in some sort of distress with the prospect of having to eat one more.

"Well, really captain, I had enough, my diet you know...."

"No, don't worry about that, I used very lean meat, and they are not good when reheated. My wife's recipe and all. No, just eat it, I know you like them."

The conversation went back and forth for a little while longer and at the end, the pilot resigned to eating yet another giant meatball. I could hear the labored swallowing and occasional gagging sounds for at least half an hour. Luckily for me, the Captain had chosen to stay at the other side of the wheelhouse with the pilot, so I was able to dispose of my ball, relatively easy, piece-by-piece, into the nearby garbage can. Half an hour later, after we had passed Ripple Shoal with a few hours of straight sailing ahead of us, the Captain disappeared.

"Oaaah, I have to go outside, get some fresh air.' The pilot moaned, "I feel sick in my stomach."

The conversation for the remainder of our watch together, definitely was poor. The pilot remained outside, both hands stretched in front of him holding the railing, his head in the wind and occasionally staggering inside to check the map, and me in a little better shape, but only marginally so. Both of us occasionally burped and we contaminated the air with odors of decaying garlic and grease, coming straight from two stomachs in turmoil.

The next day, just before the pilot left the ship, I saw him saying goodbye to the captain shaking his hand. Nothing was said about the 'delicious' meatballs but going by the hurried farewell and the big sardonic smile on the captain's face, I do understand why it has been such a long time before I saw this particular pilot back on our ship.

It was only a few months later that we experienced another memorable event with a pilot. In the mean time, we had left the beautiful Alaskan coast behind us and were back in sunny southern waters. I was preparing the bridge for departure, checking and testing every single instrument, and had just acknowledged a report from the officer at the gangway, that the pilot had boarded and was on his way up. As I was very busy, it was not until at least 20 minutes later, when the captain arrived on the bridge and asked where the pilot was, that it dawned on me that covering the distance from the gangway to the bridge shouldn't take more than 5 minutes, and using an elevator, it could be done in less than three. Even when using the stairs, a feat I yet had to see the first pilot accomplish, should have put him on the bridge by now, for his second cup of coffee. Had something happened? Before I could investigate it, the door to the bridge was opened with a considerable force and slammed against the bulkhead with a loud bang.

"Hello matie! Good to see you, Hey, you must be the captain, let me shake your hand man!"

Before our astonished captain could come up with an appropriate welcome, the boisterous and unshaven man who had entered, took his hand, and cupped it in his own and pumped vigorously, causing the poor man to spill half the coffee from a cup in his other hand. At the same time, a strong smell reminiscent of a rich variety of liquors, explained that this indeed was a very happy man.

"Let go your lines and half ahead on two engines. You got two engines don't you? Starboard your rudder."

His mouth slowly sagging, the captain looked at me and than at the man, now slumping over the instrument console, while trying to focus at the ship's helm through a pair of binoculars he was holding the wrong way around.

"I think he's drunk."

"As a skunk, smell him."

The helmsman remarked. He had walked over to the pilot, his head slightly tilted towards him, making a show smelling his breath while at the same time staying clear as much as possible. The captain seemed at a loss of how to go about this never experienced before situation. He scraped his throat a few times and blinked with his eyes when a minute later he saw the pilot slowly sagging to the floor, where he noisily fell asleep.

"We have to leave sir, it's ten past five already, the sail away party already started."

"Yes, I know..........." It would be my only time ever to see this captain at a loss of what to do. Suddenly however he came out of his spell of indecisiveness, his jaw jutted forward a bit.

"Call housekeeping."

At a loss of what housekeeping could do about the situation, I did as he requested. In the mean time he grabbed a radio and instructed the officers forward and aft to let go of the mooring lines and started to maneuver the ship out of the harbor.

"Don't need that drunk idiot to do this."

I heard him mumbling under his breath. Halfway out, the Chief Housekeeper arrived in the wheelhouse, his eyebrows raised almost to his hairline in amazement when he had to step over the pilot to reach the captain.

"Get some of your guys with a luggage trolley. Cart that guy to the pilot ladder, we have to get rid of him. A few sailors will help you there."

"Beg your pardon sir, what…?"

Slowly we started to see the hilarious aspect of it all, and with a lot of laughs the pilot was hoisted onto the little cart, normally used for suitcases, and trollied to the pilot ladder. The bosun already had installed a block and tackle and without much ceremony, a rope was tied under the pilot's armpits and he was hoisted down into his boat like a sack of potatoes. Strangely enough, nobody of the small crew on board the boat seemed to think anything strange about the whole situation and dragged the man into the tiny wheelhouse.

Again, after all these years at sea, I still do think that I have seen most of it, but I must say that I probably will not be too amazed if even more preposterous situations happen. In these times of computers and regulations, I'm very glad that we still work with human beings and that we will have to allow for all that comes with them.

ℒisa

During my years as a captain on a cruise ship, I have found out that the best way to stay relaxed and rested, is to catch brewing trouble as early as possible and deal with it immediately. Walking around, watching, talking to passengers and crew, it's amazing what one hears and sees. Things, which otherwise never would have come to my attention and which often are so important.

Happily I was chatting away to an older lady, telling her about Stockholm, our next port of call, when all of a sudden I lost all my focus. A blond girl had caught my eye, a girl I had not seen before yet and who looked beautiful.

"Yes captain, I will surely do that, take a city tour and see the city that way."

"What? Oh, yes."

With some effort, I forced myself to return to the more earthy matters and tried to say goodbye to the old lady. After a tantalizing five more minutes, she left, happy with what I had told her. To be honest, if she had talked for just one more minute, it would have ended in embarrassment, as the subject of our talk had completely slipped from my mind. I found myself standing in the main lobby of the ship, not knowing what action to take. The girl had disappeared up the staircase at the far end of the lobby minutes ago and there was no way that I would be able to catch up with her. Panicking I tried to figure out what to do. I had to see her. I managed to pull myself down from the clouds and started thinking coherently. The cruise was almost half over now. How was it possible that I hadn't seen her? To be honest, I was becoming a little aggravated with her. It would have been impossible for me to miss her during introductions, so she must have skipped that party at the beginning of the cruise.

"Silly woman, why did you not show up?" I muttered to myself.

"I beg your pardon!"

"Oh, I'm sorry madam, I was talking to myself."

I would be better off to go back to my cabin as I slowly was losing my composure. One woman was looking at me very disapprovingly already.

I sat down on my couch, wanting to see her again. But who was she, what was her name and how to find her? Leafing through the passenger list, I realized it would not do me any good, as it didn't mention if somebody was blond or good looking in the eyes of the captain.

Years at sea does, install a certain measure of common sense and the ability to think logically in a person, I had an idea. Did I not see her with another girl, and an older man and a woman? Maybe they traveled together as a family. There should be some clues to that in the passenger list. Feverishly I went through the list with 1400 names again, from front to back and around. About a hundred possibilities came up, I was becoming desperate. About 20 women sharing cabins, a few had the same surnames, but then their ages didn't match with what I had seen. Maybe, God forbid, she was married. Calm down, I told myself, and by the way, what's wrong with you?

I didn't know what was wrong with me. Over the years on these ships, one meets enough nice people, not to get excited over one only seen in a glimpse. After all, at one time it had been my fantasy to meet them, it even was one of the reasons I went for a job on cruise ships.

Straining my brain to find a way to solve my predicament, the solution suddenly popped up. The dining room manager! He should know about two girls traveling with their parents. A combination like this should stand out in a crowd of couples and friends traveling together. What was his number again?

"Yes, that's table 63, second sitting, they travel together, mother, father, a brunette and a blonde. Nice people."

My heart jumped and already I felt like winning the lottery. My brain shifted into high gear.

"Tomorrow evening, I want them invited to my table, the blonde at my right and the rest of the family somewhere else at the table, not too close by."

The dining room manager had some objections, he had some other passengers in mind, but I forced my will. After all, who is in charge?

After he realized that I would not change my mind, he decided he might as well get on my side. He started laughing and told me her name was Lisa and that she traveled with her sister and her parents. Going through the passenger list again, this time with more information to go on, I quickly found her and saw that she was a few years younger than I. Extending my little investigation a little further, using channels at the Purser's Office, I found out that she was single! Very pleased with myself, I sat back and smiled. Be calm, I told myself, she might be totally the wrong person for you and perhaps she dislikes you at first sight.

I would meet the guests invited for dinner in one of the lounges to have cocktails first and with butterflies in my stomach I dressed, shaved and brushed my teeth. Walking through the corridors and public rooms to the rendezvous, I looked in every mirror I passed to see if there was anything wrong with my appearance. Halfway down, I suddenly realized there was something I had overlooked; informing the hostess! While concentrating on the dinner seating as a whole, I had completely overlooked the seating arrangements for the cocktail party preceding it. She usually got there first to learn every guest's name so that she could introduce them properly to me, and in the process she always seated them as well, trying to match people as good as possible. This dedication to perfection, which made her one of the best in our company, at this particular time, was less than desirable to me.

To my dismay I was right; she had reserved a seat for me between two ladies at the opposite side from the girl who until now, I only knew as 'Lisa'. The two ladies were very pleased to have me sitting with them, but during the following half hour, I saw them exchanging puzzled glances. It must have been a strange experience, having the Captain giving wrong answers to otherwise simple questions and often hardly answering at all. I don't know if these ladies will ever read this, and if so, I like to offer my sincere apologies for my behavior that evening. They were two very dear people who deserved a lot more attention than I could give them.

I always had considered myself as somebody in charge. Well, not so that evening, my brain was in turmoil and did seem to short circuit every now and then. If somebody was in control, it certainly wasn't me.

Lisa talked to the people next to her and seemed to hardly notice me. It made me desperate and I cast some very dirty looks at our innocent hostess who had arranged the seats and who was clearly at a loss as to why the Captain looked at her like that. The poor girl was becoming as nervous as could be, thinking she must have done something wrong. The situation was getting a little out of hand, at least in my eyes. The hostess acting like a nervous wreck and the captain behaved like a complete fool.

Looking around me, the guests did not seem to notice that

anything was wrong. `They were probably too well mannered to show their concern.

The saying 'saved by the bell' truly did apply to me that evening. Right at the time when I had completely lost the subject of the conversation with my neighbor, the bellboy came with his gong, followed by the dining room manager. Our table was ready, he announced. It was time for me to sit next to Lisa. For the first hour I limited myself to some polite general conversation with her and the other tablemates, although I must confess that I do not remember any of them, being so preoccupied.

A wise man once said that when one wants to know a girl, look at her mother. I heeded that advise and secretly scrutinized her. She was seated conveniently far away, but close enough to talk. A nice woman with intelligent eyes and good looking too. Her father was a quiet man, very distinguished and watched me with keen eyes. I couldn't escape the feeling that he looked completely through my little deception. Later I learned that he did indeed. Lisa's sister, a very attractive girl too, had not been very fortunate with her seat assignment. To the left of her was an incredibly old gentleman, wearing malfunctioning hearing aids. He did not seem to notice who was sitting next to him, as he appeared to be primarily occupied with emptying his plate without spilling anything. A feat, I must say, he was not too successful with. On her other side, there was a young girl, as shy as children can be, who did not provide her with much diversion either. A few times she looked at me rather unhappily, making me feel a little guilty. However this disappeared immediately every time Lisa looked at me with her deep blue eyes.

Ever since, I have tried to remember what we talked about that evening, but I draw a complete blank. Whenever she spoke to me I only saw those blue eyes. She of course expected a reply and each time I answered I saw her eyes opening a little wider in surprise. With a heroic effort I pulled myself together and forced to concentrate my thoughts. Eventually I even succeeded in making a few witty remarks, that made her laugh, but even more, helped me restore my self-confidence. To be honest, I did nothing more than reciting a few standard jokes, which I knew usually got a good laugh. Over the years I have found out that when in trouble always go back to the basics and start from there. That's what I did and with success, she laughed and slowly the tension eased away.

Thinking back about that evening, I still don't know what kept me going; my self control or the two glasses of wine, as by the end of the evening, when looking at the bill, I discovered that I had more than one glass, which is proper for the man in command. On the other hand, I can argue the case that this evening, I clearly was not in command at all. Nobody was.

After dinner I asked her out, to see the show and she readily agreed. For the next evening we planned something different together, maybe something as romantic as walking the outside decks in the moonlight. Until that day I never was a romantic person at all, but suddenly, walking the decks in the moonlight with Lisa seemed to be the most desirable thing in the world to do. Well, it did not happen as she stood me up! I waited for two hours, but she never appeared. Passengers passing by, mostly couples, cast odd looks at me, the captain standing in the same place at the railing for two hours. To me, they were a sore sight, strolling in the moonlight, the exact thing that I should be doing at that very moment. The by now often mentioned moonlight started to lose much of its appeal to me, and deflated I returned to my cabin. Silly woman, I muttered.

The officer on the bridge never knew why his captain suddenly was in such a bad mood and why he took it out on him. Nothing was right; the logbook was filled out wrong, the chart was not kept correctly, he had purposely hidden my binoculars and even the coffee was lousy. I went to bed and slept very badly, only to discover the next morning that I had overslept. My mood had not improved very much and I decided not to go to the bridge, as there was too much wrong there, at least in my eyes. Walking down to the Purser's Office for a meeting, somebody called my name and turning around, I saw her.

"I'm so sorry, I took a nap last night and didn't wake up until after ten, long past the time we were supposed to meet."

It was incredible, but at that exact moment my black mood evaporated.

"Oh, that's alright, I was busy anyway."

She looked relieved that I took it so lightly and apparently was not angry with her. Inside I was a little apprehensive about the date we made for that evening, and we agreed to meet in one of the public rooms. After all, it would look extremely strange if the same couples would find the captain again standing at a railing for two hours in case she would take a nap again. Over the years I had met just too many people who make it a habit of showing up late or not at all. This time however, Lisa did show up, and walking the deck in the moonlight quickly re-established itself as a very desirable activity.

We saw each other a lot during the remainder of the cruise. She gave me her address and we started writing, even a visit followed. At the moment while writing this, I am looking at a picture of Lisa, my wife.

Later she told me that she had been as nervous as I was that first night. Much later, I told her that her invitation to dinner was not the coincidence she thought it was. Her father had suspected this the very first time he laid his eyes on me. He is a very clever man I suppose.

Lisa still likes to take a nap every now and then, and when she does I often remind her of the danger of it. A nap can easily make a person miss the most important things in life.

The Smoker

Sitting out in the sun and nurturing a nice tan is almost a must for us officers on board cruise ships. A healthy looking, darkly tanned man in uniform is what our passengers and also our company likes to see. Not in the least because of the fact that we frequently are featured in the full color brochures, advertising the joys of cruising. Invariably the best looking and the darkest tanned officer is commandeered by the film crews, told to look peppy and remove the disgust from his face. Seamen are notoriously bad actors and over the years I have been amazed to see so many of us pictured in leaflets and brochures, smiling while holding binoculars and looking genuinely interested in whatever we were told to pretend. The producers of film material must love us, as every photo session surely results in hundreds of wasted pictures.

Personally, I'm particularly bad about working up a tan. Being bald and very fair skinned, I scrupulously look for any spot of shade there is to find. When going ashore I usually can be seen dashing from one shady area to the other, carrying an umbrella to cover me when there is absolutely no protection to be found Needless to say, so far I never have appeared in any of our brochures, and honestly so, without regret from my side.

Even though the sun was shining that day, and the temperatures reached well over a hundred degrees I decided to go ashore. We had docked in the ancient city of Cartagena, Colombia. The history of the place, the combination of its unique atmosphere, mixed with the flavor of South America makes it very difficult to resist. Walking around the main square immersed in thoughts about Cortez and his conquistadors, looking at the buildings from under my umbrella, suddenly my attention was caught by some commotion going on. A few yards to my left, a man was talking very loudly, his short swaying arms punching the air above him. I have learnt that interfering in local arguments is not a prudent thing to do, interfering, certainly not in the more emotional parts of the world.

The man involved however was dressed in blue and white vertical striped pants and a pink polo shirt. This made the suspicion that he could be a guest of my ship very plausible, in addition to the fact that he carried a tote bag with our company's logo on it. A few tourists had recognized me and while doing nothing themselves to help, without so many words, they clearly expected the Captain to interfere on behalf of the now loudly yelling man.

The authority of a captain, while on board is rather extensive, ashore carries very little weight, especially when dressed in wrinkled slacks and a sweat-stained shirt. With a deep sigh I moved to the little group of agitated men, all talking and gesticulating excitedly with their arms.

"What's happening, do you need help?"

"Who are you? Did I call you? Get lost! Oh, you are the captain! Hi sir."

"I saw you had an argument and wanted to make sure you are alright."

"Can you believe it, all these guys here are smoking! It's bad for them and bad for me. The fools won't even listen."

My reluctance to interfere was well founded after all. I have never smoked myself, thanks to a father who was very explicit as to what he would do to me if I ever started. Occasionally I even ask people not to smoke when I feel it bothers others. This man had to feel very strongly about it, to start a heated conversation with some rather rough looking men, and that too in a country where virtually everybody smokes, whether it be cigarettes or other substances. After my appearance, to my relief, the men lost their interest in the argument and resumed a card game they were playing, puffing away at their cigarettes.

The next day we sailed through the Caribbean. It was a glorious beautiful day; a gentle breeze was blowing over the wooden decks, filled with people basking in the sun. Fresh air is important for a human being and I decided to go outside and in the shadow have another go at a book I had been trying to finish for a few days now. Armed with a bottle of sun block of the highest protection grade our shops had to offer, the sales clerk even had to go down and get it from her locker, I sat down under a canopy and opened the book. A deck steward came by and took my order of freshly squeezed orange juice. Life was good, sailing a blue sea, sipping a drink and reading a book. How much better could it get?

"I can't believe it! What do you think you are doing, you're killing everybody off! Being a captain does not mean you have the right to do this to me!"

A very loud and obnoxious voice shattered my peace, while at the same time attracting the interest of virtually every person sitting on the same deck.

"Yeah, don't look so innocent, I see you were smoking and yesterday you told me, you didn't. What kind of a person are you?"

Speechless I looked at him. My mouth had dropped open. Me smoking? Nonplussed I followed the accusing look in his eyes to the table I had put my drink on. There was the proof that I had smoked, an ashtray with two cigarette butts in it. Unthinkingly and not bothered by smoke being in the open air, I had sat down in the smoking section of the deck. The table I had chosen apparently was just vacated by somebody who had smoked a few cigarettes.

"Do you realize how unhealthy this is and that you will kill yourself!"

"Yes, but I wasn't smoking, somebody else..."

"Don't give me that mister, I would understand if you just admitted it, but now I don't know about you and this cruise line. How can they make people like you Captain if you don't know a lie from the truth."

"But listen..."

"No, I won't listen, you are pathetic. Look at me, I was a very heavy smoker for years, but I quit. I was coughing all the time, stinking up the house and looked terrible. Now look at me and you see a healthy happy man."

Staring at him, my initial anger started to disappear as fast as it had boiled up inside me. Rarely had I seen a more unhappy man in my life, even his health looked questionable to me, going by the look of his dark red face and the magnitude of his bulk. Finally seeing the humor of the situation I asked him to sit down with me to chat and have a drink together. His name was Bert he told me, and he was very much an anti- smoker, a fact I already had figured out. He cruised alone as his wife had passed away a few years before. Underneath the layer of tough and unpleasant veneer, I detected a very lonely man of single-minded integrity. Smoking had taken his wife and both his children and he had onlyone devotion left, to save others.

"Hey you, lady, you can't do that."

Bert suddenly sprinted away as at the far side of the deck, a woman had sat down, at least one foot on the wrong side of the boundary between the smoking and nonsmoking sections of the deck. She had lit a cigarette and just exhaled her first puff when Bert almost barged into her. I could not hear the conversation, but to my delight, I saw the lady extinguishing her cigarette and Bert patting her back as if he praised a dog who had retrieved a stick.

"She wants to stop, but never managed it," Bert told me when he returned.

"Maybe now she will, I gave her a few good hints."

We talked for about half an hour after which I excused myself, becoming increasingly tongue tied, with this extraordinary man. The conversation was exclusively about how to stop smoking and the dangers of nicotine. Walking away I saw Bert looking around the deck, his eyes searching for more addicted creatures in dire need of his guidance.

The persistent ringing of the telephone that night, next to my bed reached into the inner depths of my sleep and woke me up. Picking it up I already knew it could not be seven o'clock yet.

"Can you come to the bridge sir, we have a problem."

The duty officer did not waste any time in telling me why he needed me. Jumping out of bed, my left big toe painfully hit the dresser. Wincing I pulled my robe from a hook and limped to the bridge.

"Sir, we have a fire alarm in one of the passenger cabins and we cannot get in as the door is double locked from the inside. The telephone is probably off the hook and we need your master key to get in."

Modern ships are equipped with very different door locks than in the old days. Nowadays various levels of master keys can open certain groups of doors. Only the Captain has a key that over rides every lock on board indiscriminately. Forgetting my sore toe, I ran back to my cabin and returned with the key a few seconds later.

"It's cabin 372 sir, I already alerted a fire squad and they are on their way. Also I called the cabins next door and above 372 and they are being evacuated at this moment."

At least the officer had done what was most important and I decided to rush to the affected cabin. Normally a Captain would stay on the bridge during a fire, but so far only smoke was being reported and no real fire.

Arriving at cabin 372, I saw crewmembers rolling out hoses while others guided passengers away to clear the area. Cabin 372 was quiet and I saw no smoke coming from under the door, only a little of it filtered out through the ventilation grid at the lower part of it. With a little luck we would be in time to save whoever was inside and at the same time avoid a lot of damage and discomfort. As if I was doing a magic act, everybody held their breath when I unlocked the door and moved away to let the fire squad people open it slightly to see if there was any real fire inside. Two men wearing air masks cautiously moved in, dragging a fire hose with them.

"What the hell? What do you want? Get out!"

A collective sigh of relief could be heard from everybody around. The person inside clearly was very much alive. Although relieved, contrary to the others, I froze; as I knew that voice. It was Bert's. Shoving a few fire fighters aside I moved forward into the cabin .The scene inside, I will not lightly forget, as it was so endearing and sad at the same time. I saw Bert sitting in bed, still trying to hide the remnants of a thick Cuban cigar. An ashtray lay on the floor with ashes, cigar and cigarette butts spilled all over the chair and the dresser. The ashtray apparently had fallen down when Bert in panic had tried to stub out his cigar.

When I looked at him, I saw a hopeless look in his eyes, and slowly they filled up with tears. Without further words I told the firemen to leave the cabin. When I turned around again to Bert, he was sitting on the side of the bed, his short legs sticking out of his green, checkered pajamas. Silently he cried and looked at me again.

"I understand Bert, don't feel so bad."

At the end of the cruise, he left the ship and I never heard of him again. Thinking about him, I know he was a good man and far more human than most of us.

Phil Cassandra

A World Cruise is the ultimate in travel. After all, where else can one go on this planet? An often-remembered remark a frequent cruiser once made was; "I've been around the world 16 times now, next year I'm going somewhere else."

Only a select few are fortunate enough to have the time and the means available, to be able to go around the world in this grand style. I don't even think it's for everyone, months and months on the ship, away from home and friends. Of course there are new friends to be made and carefully selected exotic and mysterious places to be visited, but doing so alone, and at an advanced age requires a more than average will-power.

While on board, the happy few are pampered by an equally fortunate crew. Oh yes, we also consider ourselves very lucky to be on such a cruise. Crewmembers are willing to go a long way to get on, wait in some cases, even for years, and do whatever is necessary to get a place on a ship going on such a voyage. I still remember a nurse who otherwise would have stopped sailing, remained at sea for many more years, as she was promised a world cruise in the future.

Are these passengers happier than those who can only afford a short cruise? In general I don't think so. In many cases, they are older, and while leaving them with ample funds, their partner in life has gone, undertaking an even grander voyage, leaving them behind so lonely.

The cruise lines of course have recognized this and especially on the very long cruises, always provide company for those who yearn for it; somebody to talk to, play card or dance with. This company mostly consists of a group of gentlemen, who are not normal crewmembers. Oh no, they are usually signed on as 'Social Host'. They are not paid any wages, and are on board for free, provided they spend the majority of the time at sea entertaining and do some tour escorting while in port.

There is nothing gaudy about such an arrangement. The gentlemen otherwise would never have been able to afford to go on such a beautiful voyage and in many cases, they are in almost identical circumstances as those they are supposed to entertain. Except of course for a multi zeroed bank account. A true win-win situation one could say.

The cruise was not even one week old, when I heard somebody behind me, yelling out loud. "Hey, you're on the cruise again, you lucky bugger, good to see you." I turned around, and saw Phil Cassandra, one of the twelve or so social hosts we had on board.

Phil was a distinguished looking gentleman of medium length, in his early sixties with wavy gray hair. With his classic Italian features and manners, he could have fooled every one about him being a great movie star, playing in movies such as the 'Godfather'. The only challenge in his life, being a chronic shortage of funds, he ceaselessly pursued every way his mind was able to conceive, to acquire the means to support a more lavish life-style than his present meager one.

"So you're on again."

"Yeah, man, and this time I'm going to find the one."

It was common knowledge that Phil had been trying very hard to find himself somebody to support him in achieving the much grander state of affairs he longed for.

He wasn't too secretive about it either, as we often saw him sitting in a bar, discussing his chances with any willing ear. This openness probably also was the main reason for him being so unsuccessful until now. After all, many of his 'targets' as he called them, had shared the better part of their lives with men who had achieved great wealth and if nothing else, they usually were not lacking in their ability to smell a rat.

It was not until many weeks later that the rumor circulated around the ship that Phil had found himself a girlfriend and that an engagement party might be forthcoming. All of us of course eagerly awaited the sure to come invitation. Hadn't we spent many hours with him, sitting in the bar, loaning him money? Also, to a man, we were very curious who the lucky woman might be. The invitation never arrived however. Not long after these first rumors, the gossip even increased, Phil was taken of the crew list, and put on the passenger list instead. He was dating a fabulously wealthy lady, the one of suite 7314.

He would continue the cruise in the comfort of the biggest cabin on board instead of a shared one on B-deck. After that the rumors started to die down, as the information on Phil and his woman became more solid. This also killed the interest somewhat, as nobody was really interested in straight facts. By that time however, Phil had moved out of our field of interest and only rarely his name still came up during a conversation.

Just a few weeks before the end of the cruise, I ran into him again when we both were having a haircut in the ship's salon, our chairs next to each other. He looked very well; healthy and prosperous, in a shiny expensive suit. He still was his old slightly pompous self.

"I'm getting married next month, Shari and me. Yes, I knew I would find myself a woman during this cruise. She is so rich, you wouldn't believe it, must have real estate in every city on the East coast."

"Well, I must say that you look like you have it made, haven't met her yet, nor have we seen you for months."

My hope that he would get the hint of having neglected his old companions proved to be unfounded, as he wasn't even listening. He looked around him and turned towards me, the girl doing his hair had walked off to pick up some shampoo or so. With his hand, he shielded his mouth and whispered.

"My God, you should see her bank account, and she has cut her children out of her will. Can you imagine, I'm only 62 and she is 85!"

With a big smile on his face he sat back in his chair, a man in bonus, without a worry in life. I must have looked impressed, because he continued telling me about all the plans he had for the future. Taking a vacation, traveling to Europe, buying a few expensive cars and doing a lot more.

"Well you and your wife must have lots of energy, My God, it looks like you will spend half your time on the road."

"Neeh.." His hand made a dismissive move. "I'll probably go alone, she is 85 you know, and none too healthy. A cruise is about all she can do. You'll probably see us back here, next year. Same cabin of course."

True enough, almost a year later, I saw Phil again, this time together with his bride Shari sitting in her wheelchair looking as frail as the year before. He looked a little tired and shook his head when I asked him about all the travel without doubt he had done during the past year.

"Well you know, Shari was sick for a while, and then we had to visit her children the sale of some real estate had to be arranged, you know how it goes. After this cruise, I'll do some travel on my own."

"But I thought the children..."

Shari looked at me and the smile from her age-wrinkled face put a chill down my spine and left me greatly unnerved.

"Shall we go now dear? We have to meet Abi for tea in the Card room."

"Yes dear, I'll bring you."

With an audible sigh, Phil pushed the wheelchair towards the elevators. I turned around and collected my wits. Maybe the hand Phil had dealt himself was not as good as he tried to make everybody believe it was. There followed a period of many years; that I wasn't one of the chosen few who did the World cruise and sailed the Caribbean instead. To be perfectly honest, I did not regret this in the least, as there are few cruises as demanding of an officer as this one. Especially for those higher up on the promotion ladder, a level I had reached by now. In all honesty, I also should tell you that as I now was a higher-ranking officer, that same promotion had put me at the bottom of the list of those considered in my rank.

During those years, I never saw Phil or Shari, but I kept hearing about them, returning every year again, always the most expensive cabin. Exactly the style Phil had yearned for so much for so many years.

Embarkation in New York in January always is a cold affair and standing at the gangway, greeting the newly embarking guests, I did not immediately recognize the old gentleman laboring to push a wheelchair up the slightly inclining gangway. Giving it only a cursory glance, the wheelchair almost could have been empty, as one hardly could distinguish the frail unhealthy looking little figure covered with blankets inside it. The gentleman himself didn't look much better, as he strained to push the chair over a doorstep half an inch high, an expensive fur coat draped clumsily around his skinny stooped shoulders.

All of a sudden a face of many years ago started coming back to me. I looked again and suddenly it registered, and I recognized the old man.

"Phil! How are you, man, it must have been 15 years since I last saw you." Clumsily, the wheelchair stopped halfway across the threshold, the old man turned around and stared at me with rheumy uncomprehending eyes.

"I'm not sure I know you, sir."

"We sailed together years ago, when you worked here on board."

Slowly it seemed to dawn on him and fleetingly I saw a shadow of a smile on his face.

"Oh yes, yes, Nice to see you, but now I have to go and get Shari to her cabin."

Shari? Standing there, Phil had turned around and left, I did some fast calculations, mainly using my own increased age to measure the amount of years gone by since I last sailed on a World Cruise. Wasn't she 85 then? And that was 15 years ago! She must be a century old by now. I marveled at this conclusion and admired the stamina she must have to each year, still do what she had done for the past half century, making a trip around the world in luxury.

Phil and Shari seemed to keep to themselves. My function now dictated that I attend virtually every party given on the ship, which, rest assured, was a very considerable amount. I never saw them out not together and not separate either for that matter. From the hotel manager, I heard that they hardly left their cabin. That is until halfway through the cruise, when my staff captain came to me, informing me that one of our guests had passed away during the night. Her first name was Shari Cassandra.

Somehow, I expected to see Phil, but I did not, he choose not to meet anyone and stayed in his cabin.

The only time I ever saw him again was a few days later, when he left the ship in Singapore. He looked very pale and haggard and very old. He cried when he saw me. My first thought was that somehow he must have been very attached to Shari, after all they had been married a long time. I walked over to say a few comforting words, as I was one of the very few people on board who had known him from the old days, before he got rich. When he looked up at me, he could not hold out any more and started sobbing loudly.

"Fifteen years, Fifteen years I've pushed her around, did everything for her, and now she has given it all to charity."

Shaking my head, I watched him being rolled down the gangway in Shari's old wheelchair. Poor Phil, Shari outsmarting him, was the last thing he had expected.

The Lady with the Cane

"You work here?"

I turned around and saw an elderly lady with a walking cane standing behind me.

"My air conditioning is not working. You'd better come right away, too hot." Torn between our duty to provide our passengers with the perfect vacation and a succulent breakfast of crispy fried bacon and two eggs over easy on toast; I attempted to explain to her that the workings of an air conditioning system are not really within the captain's competency. Nevertheless I got up and informed her I would page an engineer to settle her problem. After fulfilling my promise I sat down again.

"Why don't you go to your cabin?" I suggested. "An engineer will be on his way." She eyed me dubiously as if I was telling her some outrageous lie.

"You can't fix it." She stated, impatiently tapping her cane against the leg of my chair. I began to lose my appetite for my sumptuously greasy breakfast, my once a week sin that I had been looking forward to so much. And then, all of a sudden she yelled across the restaurant. "Over here!" She raised her cane simultaneously, tipping over my glass of buttermilk in the process. She seemed to address an aged gentleman who approached in an electric wheelchair.

Slowly her loud voice and lively behavior started to arouse the curiosity of the other passengers. After all, an elderly lady waving about her cane and shouting at the top of her voice is not an everyday occurrence. Some of the more enterprising men having breakfast at the tables surrounding us looked suspiciously at me. Was that guy bothering that nice old lady? Why else would she be screaming? The man in the wheelchair managed to stop his vehicle just a little too late and bumped into my table.

"You're the engineer." He observed. "I saw you yesterday fixing the temperature in the cabin next to us. Now you're giving us their hot air. I want you to fix it now."

I realized the futility of my attempts to save my breakfast and the necessity to salvage the rest of the morning. I got up with an audible sigh and my stomach protested against such a sudden halt to its weekly indulgence.

"Alright, I will see what I can do, what's the number of your cabin?"

She was not listening to me and instead she looked around her, triumph showing in her eyes. Single handedly she had managed to pry this engineer from his chair and press him into action. Then she turned to me.

"My cabin?" She asked vaguely.

"Yes your cabin, you told me that your air conditioning needs fixing."

For a few seconds I hoped she had forgotten all about her problem and that my breakfast, still warm, could still be saved. This was in vain though.

"Come with me young man." She ordered.

The man in the wheelchair, who I correctly presumed to be her husband, tried to follow us but was only partly successful as some how a tip of the tablecloth had wrapped itself around one of the electric controls on his armrest, which resulted in a very unwanted command to the electric motor. Without warning he rushed forward at break neck speed, barely missing a steward carrying a fully loaded tray. I froze, seeing this all happening not five yards away from me. At the same time, I could not help making a one sided comparison between his chair and one of those electric cleaning carts I had seen on the airports as both left a clean path behind them. His wife sensing that the general attention in the restaurant had shifted from her to her husband became clearly annoyed.

"Herb, stop that!"

As if by magic, at that very moment, Herb managed to un tangle the tablecloth from his control panel and stopped in his tracks. It was not a moment too soon as he had rapidly approached an enormous ice carving of an American Bald Eagle that sadly stood at the entrance of the restaurant, dripping away, in ever-increasing temperatures. I, in the mean time, welcomed this commotion, as it gave me a chance to sneak away from the scene. There were only a few feet left between me, and the entrance to the kitchen. Optimism in life has always been my main daily support. This time however I would need more than that, for after instructing Herb not to play around and to behave himself, she discovered that I was missing.

"You stop, come back!" She yelped when she noticed me just before I could vanish. I began to severely resent her calling me 'hey you' all the time. After all, as a captain of an impressive passenger vessel I feel I deserve a little more respect. Quite possibly she might have felt the same, if only she would have believed that indeed I was the captain.

Although the fourth of July was still months away, we left the restaurant as in a parade. The first in line were two stewards to open the doors, eager to guide such a destructive person to another part of the ship, then me, being driven out like a cow on her way to the market with the lady waving her cane behind me, then her husband, sulking and muttering about wheelchair manufacturers in general and this one in particular. The last in the parade was the dining room manager, making sure that we were truly leaving.

While we waited for an elevator, I again asked her for her cabin number.

"I hear you," she snapped and looked at me as if I had just made her a very indecent proposal.

"Well, if I have to fix your air conditioning, we must go to your cabin. So tell me where it is, we can ride the elevator to your deck."

"Beats me...Herb, Herb what was our cabin again?"

Meanwhile, I was getting severe misgivings about this Sunday. Its start had not been up to standards and it would probably rain too. Herb was still struggling with the controls of his wheelchair and seemed unable to switch his brain into producing his cabin number. He blandly informed me that he did not know. My feelings towards the old lady slowly started to change from annoyance to compassion. She did not look too formidable anymore and I noticed that the cane with which she had threatened me only minutes before, was trembling pitifully. They needed help that was clear to me, all the help I could give them, if not by fixing their air conditioning then at least by me finding their cabin for them.

"Don't worry, we will find your cabin, tell me your name and I'll call the Purser to check the manifest for your cabin."

They both looked at me.

"I'm Herb," Herb finally stated. He had given up trying to take his wheelchair apart and now focused his attention on the buttons of the elevator. The lady looked at me open mouthed and slowly raised her cane again, as if ready to hit me. I decided that my duties did not include being struck and grabbed the end of it and slowly forced it back to the floor.

"I don't know..." She said. Looking into her eyes, I saw

they suddenly reflected a sea of misery.

It must be pouring outside I thought grimly, as what else could I expect on a day that started like this. Then a brilliant idea flashed through my mind and inwardly I congratulated myself. Herb's wheelchair, I saw was a rental from our infirmary, owned by the ship. The nurses would know to whom and which cabin it belonged. A telephone was nearby.

"Good morning, infirmary, how may we help you?"

As usual, our lead nurse was on duty already and answered the phone. I started to explain the situation to her but only after telling her less than half of it, I heard her exclaim loudly. "You found them! We were looking for them all over the ship; their daughter lost them both. They have not taken their medicine yet. Where are you?" Very relieved I informed her of my location, and even before I put down the phone, I heard excited voices. Mom and dad were found.

Herb had decided that he was bored and while I was on the phone he had called up an elevator. Whether he assumed that the elevators on the ship were solely for him to use and nobody else, or that the lack of his morning medicine influenced his ability to both watch the controls of his wheelchair and the way he was going, I do not know. Fact was that when the doors opened, Herb gave 'Full Speed Ahead', to use a nautical term. Hungry people usually are not the most patient ones and those inside the elevator, ready to exit into a food filled restaurant were no exception. Expecting to leave a cramped little place to have breakfast and instead almost being crushed by a charging wheelchair did not go too well with them. Vigorous protests, some from angry people and from others in pain came from the little cubicle. Taken aback, Herb managed to reverse and leave the elevator even faster that he had entered it, hobbling over the same toes twice.

"There you are; why did you run off?" A young woman and

our lead nurse had finally arrived.

"He does not want to fix our air conditioning, I asked him over and over! Let me get his name, I'll report him to the captain, that will teach him a lesson."

The lady, whose name and cabin number I never learned was led away by the nurse. Herb followed in his wheelchair. Their daughter later wrote me a letter, how great their time had been on board our ship. Her parents had talked about nothing else for months after they returned home. She thanked me for my patience. I could not read her name and the signature, but this did not bother me at all. I prefer to remember her mother as 'The lady with the cane'

The Dinner Party

One of the nicest things about working on cruise ships is the fact that one can have his wife sail with him. Even other family members can come at regular times. Yes, I know, the perk also exists on cargo ships, but then, what can we offer our loved ones on such a ship? A container terminal many miles from the closest form of civilization, the company of the same fifteen or twenty people for months at a time and a very limited space to move around while on board.

Accommodations on board cargo ships are often far more generous than those on cruise ships, but once outside the cabin, there's nothing but the great expanse of the ocean. Being in the middle of the ocean is a pacifying and often humbling experience, but on the other hand, being there for weeks at a time with little else for diversion than a video and a few books becomes boring after a while. It can be so for us, the crew, and it is doubly so for family.

I have taken my wife on numerous cruises and even my mother, brother and sister have come along at times. The experience of having them on board is great, an eye- opener for both sides. Finally they understand what this type of work is all about and how stressful it can be at times. No longer, when at home you see the vague, staring, uncomprehending look in their eyes, when telling about life at sea. It's not only that family can sail with us; occasionally friends can also come. Granted, they have to pay their fare, but usually the cruise line will offer a discount at the times of the year when passenger counts are low and space is easily available.

It was about halfway through our cruise of the Baltic when I decided that it would be very nice to invite a few close friends to my cabin for dinner, something I rarely do. I have always felt a little awkward, asking the maitre d' for special treatment. When looking at the duties of the dining room personnel, it is difficult to ask for extra service, as they are so busy already coping with their normal workload. This time I decided it should be different as it was a very special cruise for me. Amongst the passengers were not only my mother and my sister, but also Simon and Cathy, two people whose friendship goes back to my very early days on cruise ships. On top of it all, Daniel, my long time friend and security officer was on board and due to go on a vacation at the end of that cruise. All together, enough reasons to throw a little party, I thought.

The maitre d' didn't make any objections at all. He actually stated that as so far he had not had any special requests from me so he was willing to accommodate my request. That his choice of words did not exactly please me very much must have been very apparent, as I saw his face registering alarm, and hurriedly he corrected himself. Of course he would honor any request from my side, no matter when and how. That was better and I left it at that. Organizing my little party was easy enough, at least it seemed that way. After all, a few telephone calls should do the trick, shouldn't they? Just give them the time and the amount of people attending and Voila!

Our executive chef must have been very bored repeatedly preparing his regular weekly menu, as he jumped to the idea with excessive enthusiasm. He assured me that he would serve the best of the best, he would let his fantasy go wild and put a dinner on my table worthy of the best restaurants in Paris, he would outdo Maxim's, he would...I stopped him. Our French Chef was known for his attempts to use the English language pretty much in the same way as he would his native tongue. Somehow however, it always sounded and looked funny, when Francois expressing the feelings of a creative Frenchman in a language so much more formal than his own. While the words he used were definitely English, the actions of his arms and hands, with which he drew a picture in the air of how his creations would look, were decidedly French. While not completely understanding the combination of the two, I decided to leave it with him. I surely wouldn't have to worry about the quality of the dinner. I didn't even offer the slightest suggestion, just let the chefs create something and it would be good.

Instructing my cabin steward about the upcoming culinary event in my stateroom proved to be a little more daunting. A situation not made any easier by the fact that the poor man had joined the ship only a few weeks before, and was on his first assignment. If I understood him well, I believe that before he had worked as a kitchen hand in a local hotel, somewhere in the inner lands of India. Contrary to what most passengers believe, namely that the captain always has the most experienced help on the ship, reality often is different. Usually we are left with the newest crewmember, most in need of training. I even have the, probably true, suspicion that this is done on purpose. Let the captain teach him the job and then we will transfer him to a guest section, the chief housekeeper must think.

The concept of an American table setting totally eluded poor Akim. Why was such a complex array of cutlery next to the plates, two knives, three forks two spoons, and other accessories necessary? To him they were completely redundant. Could not every imaginable dish be eaten with bare fingers? Under less formal circumstances, I could agree to a certain extent, as I felt a little ill at ease explaining the necessity of every piece of equipment to him. After all I wasn't too sure

about the purpose of all this silverware either. Never exactly
having made a study of proper table etiquette, I always had
limited myself, cutlery concerned, to the fact that one starts
using it, working from the outside to the inside.

My rising anxiety of the coming evening was somewhat
relieved by the maitre d' who told me he would assign an extra
steward for that evening. Bringing up the food from the ship's
kitchen to my cabin was too much of a job for one person
alone. Not so much the amount of food to be carried, but more
so the distance to be covered. Not knowing he embarrassed me
greatly, he looked at the table and while shaking his head, he
quickly adjusted most of the settings, that I so painstakingly had
set out in front of Akim. Well, at least nothing could go wrong
anymore.

At seven thirty that evening we all gathered in my sitting
room for a glass of wine and chatted about past sailings
together. While we all knew each other, we never had been on
one ship at the same time. Life on ships is like that. It brings
people together so that they can become friends. Then for
some cruel reason, separates them again and nobody knows
when they will meet again. In most cases it's fine with me,
after all, the same has happened for many years and I'm used
to it. Working relations after all are only that. Of course there
are always exceptions, especially with those who become
friends. Often it is difficult not seeing them again for years
and in some cases forever. One can visit each other at home
while on vacation, but that somehow does not happen a lot. In
this business, visiting friends made on board very often would
mean traveling to the other side of the world.

My steward had dressed up in a freshly dry cleaned uniform and also his temporary assistant looked sharp. The table
setting was just beautiful, crystal wine glasses, starched white
napkins, candles and sterling company. In one smooth move,

like a professional sommelier, Akim uncorked a bottle of a seven-year-old French wine. Our chef had recommended it as being the best his country had to offer and had tears in his eyes when he described the taste to me.

While opening the bottle, Akim had looked very professional, but it became obvious that the crash course in table serving he had received that afternoon, was nothing more than that, a crash course. With an expectant smile on his face, he practically turned the bottle upside down and filled my glass to the brim with foaming wine.

Hoping that nobody had noticed this blatant breach of etiquette, I smiled and my hand went to the glass, wanting to keep at least a semblance of protocol in place. Should I still take a sip of the wine and make a little show of tasting it? We all know that doing two things at the same time is not a good idea. While I was bringing the very full glass to my mouth, to my dismay I saw that Akim did not wait for my approval of the wine. He continued to fill up every one's glass, including my mother's, ignoring her statements, of not wanting any alcoholic beverages.

The need of going through the movements of tasting and approving the wine not being necessary anymore, I decided it would be better to take a good swig, to bring the amount of wine in the glass down to a safer level. This turned out to be an error which was set straight the moment I took the sip.

Which was more worse, the taste of the wine, that had gone bad, very likely a long time ago, or the feeling in my mouth of what must be a completely disintegrated cork, pieces of which must have been hidden in the foam, I honestly can't remember. Returning the wine into the glass was not a good option, as I surely would have spilled half. A desperate dash for the toilet, creating considerable consternation amongst my table companions, was the only option.

Keeping up appearances was rather difficult for the next half hour, as until that moment I never had appreciated how bad spoiled wine really can be. Rarely had my taste buds receive such a blow and the first course, our chef had so lovingly prepared, suffered accordingly.

The first course was beautiful, at least, in my case, by the looks of it. Our culinary experts had gone out of their way in creating a fabulous plate. With a proud gesture, the chef even gave me the recipe. Later when I tried it at home myself, honesty makes me tell you, that I did not get much further than a rating of 'barely edible' from my wife. The fact that coffee was served together with the appetizer puzzled me mildly but not pretending to have any culinary insight, I put this to our chef surprising us with a new creative way of combining various flavors.

The kitchen personnel having gone out of their way, somehow also applied to the steward assigned to help out, and literally so. Service noticeably slowed down after the first course, maybe he got lost. Actually it wasn't too bad and the company was great and nobody seemed to notice. I probably was a little over sensitive. But after a certain point in time I started to become a little annoyed. After all, I was assured to have the best meal and the best service, and up till, that moment I had not asked for anything special. What was so difficult about it? I pulled myself together and forced a smile, I had to devote my attention to my company, as they deserved to have a good time.

The main course, the menu told us was a steak, and not a normal steak either. The Chef had needed three full lines on the menu to describe it in French, hence my great expectations and my even greater annoyance when after waiting for what seemed to be an eternity, the steward showed up empty handed.

"I waited for half an hour in the kitchen, but nobody knew

anything about it."

"What? I arranged it with the Chef myself, let me call."

Before I could get to the phone, it started to ring.

"Captain."

"Do you still want your steak or what, by now it's as dry as shoe leather? It's the last time I go out of my way for you."

A very annoyed Chef in his creative fury had forgotten whom he was talking to, but it didn't matter, as I barely heard him.

"What do you mean, the steward has been waiting for it for half an hour."

"Yes." The steward wailed, standing behind me. "I waited for half an hour at the Grills."

"At the grills, you idiot."

Again, hearing the steward in the background, the chef was forgetting that it was the Captain holding the phone to his ear.

"I told your boss to pick it up at my office."

It took me more than 10 minutes to pacify the chef and convince him that also with regards to his future career, he should make another attempt in creating his masterpiece. Maybe not too diplomatically I agreed with him that the communication from the maitre d' left a lot to be desired too. I should not have said this of course. The poor man, especially after having been told by a gleeful chef, that the captain backed his opinion, felt it as a personal attack.

"I'm always very explicit as to what I want from my people sir, never is there any doubt."

"So why is the service so slow this evening? Thinking of it I haven't seen the extra guy you sent to help out, for at least an hour."

The maitre started to stutter and got red in the face. Maybe I was a little too hard on him.

"Sir, I know he is new, but I told him very clearly what was expected of him, he should keep assisting till after he had served the coffee, nothing could go wrong there."

The man was right, correct instructions could only be followed up correctly. ......

"What did you say? He could go after serving the coffee?"

"Yes, that's what I told him."

"But he put coffee on the table together with the appetizers."

If possible, the maitre turned another degree redder in the face, and made some gurgling sounds. Abruptly he turned around and left. Outside I heard him yell at the top of his voice and it did not end till I heard a door slam closed. Speechless we looked at each other and suddenly like a command had been given, we started to laugh. We kept laughing till the tears came and our stomachs ached. Simon spilled half a mouth of wine into his napkin just to avoid choking on it and Daniel, the security officer, unknowingly put his elbow in his plate, still half filled with a cream sauce.

We barely had time to straighten our faces when help arrived. The maitre d, not wanting any more mistakes to happen, had summoned all the help available. Those of you, who have taken a cruise before, will know that such can be considerable. Soon it was apparent that there is such a thing as too much help. When being asked by three different stewards if one needs pepper on his steak and wine being poured almost continuously, even after having taken only a sip or two, then a safe conclusion is to say that someone is overdoing it slightly.

The realization of overkill also dawned on the maitre d' himself, when after trying to fill up my glass again, from which I hadn't even taken one sip, he discovered that the bottle he had so lovingly opened only a minute before and which he tipped over my glass to fill it up once again, was emptied already by a zealous steward. The poor man almost broke down when he saw my face, red already; change into an even darker tone. I should have told him that this was not caused by anger. It came from a complete inability to do anything but keeping my breath and hope he would go away before I exploded. I saw that the others were in the same situation as me. We all marveled at the fact that so many things could go wrong at one dinner. By that time, my earlier anger had totally evaporated into resignation. After all, our situation was funny to the extreme.

The poor maitre d' and his staff, including the chef did not see the humor of this at all. They were embarrassed to their bones.

Like said earlier, often we do not sail on the same ship for many years. This also happened to the maitre d'. It has been years since I have seen him, and I'm sure that it's fine with him and doesn't look forward to working with me ever again. There must be a little devil in me though, as I would enjoy seeing him and casually ask to organize a dinner party for me.

Mr. Dunlop

It's not too often that I check the passenger list before
departing for a new cruise. This time however I did and to my
delight I saw the name 'Robert Dunlop' appearing on it.
According to the information, Mr. Dunlop would sail with us
for the next two cruises in a row. I have known Robert for so
many years, that painfully I realized that both of us were getting older. Mostly one sees the aging process ravaging others,
without being aware that the same is happening to oneself.
Not so with Robert, who seemed to get younger every time
we met. He was an old English gentleman in the true sense of
the word. In all the years he sailed with us as a passenger, I yet
had to hear him complain or use offensive language in front of
anyone. He was always correct, happy and cheerful. When
Robert expressed his very strong disapproval of a situation or
a person, his eyes might betray him, but never his mouth. He
would just state that he did not care for him or her. I made sure
he would find a note from me in his cabin inviting him for a
chat and a drink.

Somebody knocked on my door and thinking it was my
steward, I bellowed,

"Come in!"

"Hello Hans, so nice to see you. How are your family and
your wife?"

Robert Dunlop had come aboard a little early, not yet
expected, but welcome anyway. We sat down for a short talk,
I was busy and he still had to unpack. He only came to pay his
respects, he said and would come back later. After he had left,

I sat back and smiled. Paying his respects. It should be the other way around and I should be paying my respects to him. His refreshing company was so rare that it had to be treasured whenever he was around. I counted back the years; he must be in his late eighties now. Still standing erect, still looking clean and…still a ladies man.

The first time I met him was about fifteen years ago, when we did a world cruise together. We met in a bar on board and started a conversation. What immediately impressed me was his keen eye for beautiful women. He simply didn't miss any. The subject we were talking about, I can't remember, but suddenly Mr. Dunlop seemed to lose interest a little. The Chief Officer walked by with a ravishing looking girl at his side. Mr. Dunlop, while he made some futile attempts to keep to the subject, discreetly watched her moving away from him. With a visible effort he refocused on me and saw that I was smiling.

"Well, what does one say to that, definitely appealing would be my description, what?"

I could do nothing but agree, the girl was dashing and I knew that the Chief Officer had been trying to get her attention for the last few days. As it looked, he was gaining some headway, as they seemed to be headed for the outside decks, most likely to take a romantic stroll.

"Well, let's take another snifter." Mr. Dunlop said, calling the waitress.

"This glass is one of the few special treatments I ask for, brought it myself. Waterford Crystal you know. Definitely don't like to drink malt whiskey from a plain glass. I suppose it's alright to drink water from it, but not a good whiskey."

We chatted for another half hour before we heard the bell-boy going around with his gong, announcing dinner was being served. Mr. Dunlop got up and after a 'see you tomorrow' he walked of.

The next day I did not see Mr. Dunlop at all, but well a cruise ship is big. Enough not to meet people for sometimes days in a row and Mr. Dunlop hated to impose on us.

Then after two days I began to wonder and asked around. Amazingly enough, when questioned nobody could give a satisfactory answer. Some thought they had seen him yesterday and other this morning. Nobody could give me a definite time and I started to worry, after all he was not young anymore and traveling all alone. Later again, I decided to have a look myself and see if I could find him. When walking around, passing the dining room, I saw his usual spot near the window empty and being at a loss of what to do, I looked around the room. Across, at the other entrance of the restaurant I saw the Chief Officer, who looked a little agitated, his face all flushed staring into the room. Following the direction of his gaze, I suddenly felt relieved. There sat Mr. Dunlop. He was talking to somebody who I could not see from my position. Well, I wasn't interested in the other person; at least Robert seemed to be fine.

I had a few hours to kill before going on duty, and was unsure if I should ask the Chief Officer out for a drink. After all the man had not been too friendly to me ever since I joined the ship. A little relation repair would do me good I decided. To my delight, he agreed and we sat down in one of the lounges. I ordered a Coke and he a cognac, which surprised me a little.

"I thought you didn't drink and now suddenly a cognac."

He looked at me and I swear I could hear his teeth gnashing.

"That friend of yours, that Dunlop guy. He sits in the dining room with Peggy. Right now that I have a few hours to spend with her, she decides that she likes him better than me."

He finished his cognac in a gulp and ordered another one.

"What? He is with her? I can't believe it. Come on, he probably just has dinner with her."

He didn't listen and gloomily peered in his glass.

" Don't like that guy. He is so smooth, the women practically drool all over him when he talks to them. Well, I'm off to bed, might as well turn in early, there's nothing else for me to do."

In my position, Second Officer at that time, it would have been very stupid to laugh, but it was extremely difficult to hide even the smallest smile. He left and just as I finished my drink and was getting up to leave as well, Mr. Dunlop and Peggy walked in and sat down with me. Of course, only after he had asked if this would be allright. From close by, Peggy was even more stunning than I remembered from a few days ago. Little make up, bright blue eyes and a very good conversationalist. Careful not to get caught between Mr. Dunlop as a guest and the wrath of the Chief Officer, we made polite conversation. Suddenly Robert Dunlop sat up straight, looking at his watch.

"Good heavens, it's 11 p.m. already, way past my napping time, could you please excuse an old man who needs his sleep."

We both got up and wished him a good night and sat down again after he left.

Peggy told me that he had asked her if he could join her for dinner. She had enjoyed her conversation with this delightful gentleman immensely. Now she was waiting for Peter, the Chief Officer with whom she had a date. I almost choked on the last of my drink, knowing that Peter had gone to bed at least an hour ago. Should I call him? Better not. A man woken up from his first sleep is never the best conversationalist, a fact I can testify to be correct from my own experience. I smiled. This actually was very funny. If Peter only knew! Secretly I decided to land the blow on him during coffee time tomorrow morning, and....

"What are you laughing about?"

I straightened my face.

"Nothing, just something that happened this afternoon."

"You got a nice smile."

"Yes, I know…eh, what?"

"I said that you have a nice smile," she sighed looking at her watch, "I don't think Peter will show up, maybe he has forgotten." Nothing was less the case than that, I knew, but instead of commenting on it, I nodded vaguely. Better not to get into that subject.

"The late movie starts in ten minutes, care to join me?"

Danger signals started flashing through my head, if the Chief Officer was mad with Mr. Dunlop, so be it, there was little he could do to him. With me however it was a different case altogether. The man for some reason held a grudge against me already and going to the movies with a girl I knew he was after, would not be the cleverest move I could make. Keeping it discreet was not an option either, as by that time I had been on cruise ships long enough to know that it was absolutely impossible to keep such a thing a secret.

"I would love to but I have to be on duty at that time."

This actually was the truth even though saying it almost hurt me physically. For a fleeting moment I toyed with the idea of asking her out the next evening, but again for my future it would be better not to go into that direction. Needless to say, the Chief Officer was totally unsuccessful that cruise and so was Mr. Dunlop for that matter. Robert simply enjoyed the company; he was not into playing games.

Years later, when I had become Captain and Robert and me sailed the South American coast, I told him what had happened between him and the Chief Officer. It amazed him greatly. He was never aware that he was such a serious threat, certainly not when competing with men less than half his age.

"Oh Hans, you give me such a laugh."

Later that evening he told me about his life, that had been

far from easy. Robert had worked until in his seventies. Starting in the thirties operating a small butcher shop with his father and slowly expanding, at one time owning eight of them.

"Those were difficult times," he told me, "we had to economize on everything."

He laughed when he mentioned his father's strategy to save even more.

"More bread in the sausages Robert, more bread."

The increasing amount of bread and the equally decreasing percentage of meat had made his customers complain bitterly.

"Robert, what do we have to put on our sausages, mustard or marmalade?"

Robert survived and now after many years and long hours of hard work he had become a prosperous man, able to cruise for about three months each year. One of our best loved passengers.

A few months ago, he showed me pictures of his house in Kent in England. A beautiful cottage with a gorgeous garden and a thatched roof He looked sad when he told me about his never born children and a wife who left him for his best friend, now more than 25 years ago.

Robert still cruises and we are friends. For me he is an example of what a true gentleman should be like. Thinking about him, I hear his voice.

"Count your blessings Hans, count your blessings, I certainly do count mine."

The Strike

At least ten times on each cruise, passengers ask me what my favorite place is in the world. What place I would like to return to, and where I would like to sail best. Such questions are almost always very difficult to answer, as I have many fond memories of places all over the world, and for reasons as diverse as could be. My answers also depend on the person, making the inquiry, as there is a certain responsibility here. More often then not, by asking me, there is a hidden desire for good advice. A young couple with small children would not be well guided by me telling them to take a world cruise, and equally, an elderly man and woman, would be slightly disappointed to be told to go hiking in the Himalayas.

Memories of course are very personal and one sided, and often what one remembers with pleasure is another person's horror. The real danger of giving advice based on memory, certainly if a considerable time has elapsed, is that our memories seem to delete the bad experiences and cling only to the good ones.

I always feel most comfortable giving the advice to go cruising. An industry I know more about than most and I can vouch for the fact, that a cruise is very well liked, by the overwhelming majority of our guests. We are trying very hard to give our passengers a good time. It's our business to bring pleasure to all those on board and the captain will do almost anything in his power to achieve this goal. Often enough, I have even seen captains bending some rules and taking personal risks to get what he needs for his guests. Often enough he does get what he wants, although not always in an easy way.

It was a beautiful morning as we approached Puerto Vallarta in Mexico. The cruise, which had started in Acapulco, so far had gone without a flaw. I was standing on the navigation bridge as we approached the pilot station, just outside the harbor entrance, when a frown slowly began to form on my face. We had been in Puerto Vallarta often enough, but today things seemed a little different. It looked so quiet. I couldn't detect any activity beyond the harbor entrance or on the dock. Also, shouldn't the pilot boat have come out to meet us by now?

Puzzled about this and listening on the ship's radio, I only caught a few words of the conversation going on between the duty officer and the port authorities. One remark made me turn around at the same moment the officer put down the radio. He looked at me, his expression boding little well.

"They're on strike sir. The mooring line handlers and the pilots just decided to stop working. Apparently something has been going on for weeks, the agent told me, but this morning it all blew up."

"So we can't get in."

My mind already started working at full speed. Was there perhaps an alternative port nearby, or could we get the passengers ashore in another way.

"Maybe we can anchor sir, and bring them ashore with our tenders, we did it in the past."

It was true, we had anchored at Puerto Vallarta a good many times. Anchoring normally would be a perfect second choice. Dubiously I peered out of the windows, a heavy swell was running across the anchorage. It would make the transfer of passengers from the ship into the tenders much too dangerous. No, tendering was not an option at all today. Now what?

"Why are we going so slow, where's the pilot boat?"

I turned around and looked at the staff captain who had come on the bridge. His mouth was wide open and he was stifling a big yawn and rubbing his forehead. Fred and I had sailed together for many happy years. 'Fred can do', was his nickname throughout our fleet. Never in my life, have I worked with a man with a more positive outlook on life. He was known for his optimism and his total disregard for any obstacles.

"They're on strike." I replied sourly. "We'll probably have to cancel our call."

Mentally I had started to prepare myself how to explain all of this to our passengers. Already, I could see my carefully planned day go up in smoke. Having upset guests wanting to talk to me all day was certainly going to be no pleasure.

"On strike, who and why?"

"How should I know, they just told us and now we are stuck out here. I better prepare an announcement. Get me the Cruise Director."

"Ho ho, wait a minute, why don't we go in anyway. We can do it without a pilot, its probably allowed as long as we don't go alongside the pier. We just anchor inside, no swell there, so no danger, no problem."

I looked at him and shook my head. Typical of Fred to come up with such an idea. Everything in his mind had an easy solution. Not this time though.

"Yea nice, anchoring in that tiny little inner harbor, and what about the stern swinging around. Did you think of that? We'll end up on the rocks with your ideas."

Fred was quiet, a small frown clouding his face. Suddenly the frown was gone and with a big smile and his arms spread out in triumph.

"No problem, we anchor the bow and then we just put mooring lines ashore from the back of the ship to that fishing boat dock we saw last cruise, and then she won't swing."

"Alright mister 'Can do', and how will we get our lines ashore? It's at least 500 feet and we don't have line boats since the lines men are on strike too."

The smile disappeared again and his shoulders stooped. I could see his brain working overtime. I think that he felt a heavy burden on his shoulders. If ever there was a time he had to prove he was able to live up to his nickname, this was it.

"Line boats, let me think, where can we get some boats, maybe..."

We looked at each other, and simultaneously were struck by the same idea. Fred was the first to voice it.

"Our lifeboats! We can use one of them. Told you it was possible."

Optimism is a nice character trait and in most cases is a beautiful and contagious thing. The circumstances of having to find a solution to our dilemma, made me to look at the world through Fred's glasses; a world where the sun was always shining, but not a world big on caution. Maybe I should have thought twice, but as it was, Fred finding all these solutions, all in a row, seemed to me the answer to my problems.

Our agent contacted us on the radio, and when informed about our intentions, he protested vaguely. More, I suspected, to be on record in case something went wrong, so everybody would know that he had 'told us so', than for any other reason. I'm sure that he was secretly relieved by my decision, as once he had told me that most of his family owned shops in town and depended on the business from the ships.

Maneuvering the ship, stern first, into the tiny harbor was no problem at all. The same, I am sad to say, did not apply to most of the actions I observed afterward. Lowering a lifeboat into the water with a full landing party, under command of our Security Officer, was a routine practiced numerous times during drills. It went as smooth as I could wish for. After that, came the part, which was a little less easy and of course, never practiced before. I should have thought about this before we started, but what can one say?

From experience, having observed numerous drills, every captain knows that a lifeboat is about as nimble in her handling as an old fashioned battleship, and probably even less so. While we were dropping the anchor, which is usually done with some backward movement of the ship, I saw the lifeboat getting very close to the aft part of our vessel. A moment later, to my consternation, it even disappeared from my view completely! I had to stop the ship, and fast, a disaster could happen. Instantly I pushed the engine levers from dead slow astern to more than half ahead to stop us from possibly running the lifeboat down.

The effects were spectacular. Only moments later, I saw the boat appearing again in the wash of the propeller water, pushed by more than 30.000 horses. That the whole operation was still executed without flaws would be the overstatement of the year. The erratic movements, of the little craft in the foaming water, showed that her helmsman had totally lost his focus.

Fred also noticed that his plans seemed to have developed a serious flaw and he started to yell instructions into his radio. This in turn immediately showed the next flaw in his plan, as the security officer did not seem to be able to hear his radio above the loudly puffing lifeboat engine, running at full power. The lack of attention, shown by the Security Officer, of course also might have been caused by the fact that the poor man had just fallen flat on his face, as the boat hit the pilings of the dock.

Fred's wild jumping around, gesturing with his arms, was slightly embarrassing, as quite a number of guests were observing us from the deck above. Eventually, his frantic movements did catch the attention of the engineer in the boat. We saw him motioning to the helmsman, and we saw the angry puffs of smoke coming from the old fashioned exhaust pipe of the lifeboat, lessen. Now it would be possible to communicate with less engine noise. Fred however, had passed the stage of talk, and had moved into a yelling mode.

"Get a line in that boat, don't play around any longer we don't have all day." He howled in his radio, his perennial smile by now had turned into an ugly grimace. Whether his order was reasonable or not, did not seem to matter. We saw the boat shooting forward and to my great relief, a few minutes later, it headed for the dock, a heavy mooring line attached to her bow, and draped across her top. At last things started to shape up.

"Hey, ho stop, not so fast, I can't pay out this fast." A kind of a panic sounded in the voice of the officer in charge of the mooring party at the stern of the ship.

The engineer in the boat did not share the panic with the officer at the stern; this little trip in the lifeboat most likely was welcomed by him as a nice diversion from his daily routine. That there is a danger having a boat sailing away from an object, faster that a line can be paid out, with this same line attached to both clearly did not occur to him.

With a dry mouth, I saw the little drama unfolding before my eyes. The mooring line, with the strength of more than a hundred tons, did not have trouble at all stopping the lifeboat dead in its tracks.

Two things happened simultaneously. The least important one of the two was that our security officer fell flat on his face for the second time in less than ten minutes. The other was, that in full view and to the great hilarity of more than a thousand passengers watching the procedure, the engineer, with a shrill scream was swept overboard by the suddenly tight mooring line.

Fred and I were holding our breath, but after a few seconds, the engineer's head popped up. To show us that he was well and alert, he shook his fist at the officer on deck aft, and shouted some insults at the poor man, which because of the distance I could not understand. The sudden applause of the hundreds of passengers watching the proceedings with great interest, made it clear to me that he had used some colorful words to describe his dislike of the man he held responsible for his embarrassing predicament. The crew in the boat, it seemed, had not even noticed the disappearance of one of them as without further ado, they continued their way to the dock. The line had finally been paid out and they had a mission to accomplish. The engineer, seeing the boat go, seemed to take his situation in a philosophical way and turned around and swam for a little beach near the end of the dock.

Focusing again on the lifeboat, I saw that she had reached the dock where we wanted to put our lines at, and I waited for someone to get ashore. But the activity amongst the landing party had died down and nobody seemed to move. Fred had seen it too and grabbed his radio again.

"What's happening, bring that line onto the dock. What are you waiting for?"

"It's pretty high sir." Came the voice of the Security Officer. "Must be over 20 feet or more."

"Well, climb up and lower a small rope to pull up the mooring line, I see a ladder from here."

After a short while, the Security Officer, hesitantly came back on the radio.

"Can't find a line sir. Now what."

"Well, wrap the mooring line around your back and climb that ladder yourself. You always told me how tough you were with your Marine back ground, live up to it now and don't talk, just get that line ashore."

"But sir, that was thirty years ago, I mean that ladder is straight up and pretty rusty. I'm not even talking about that rope, full of grease and I'm in my white uniform.... and..."

Fred finally completely lost his temper and seemed ready to eat his Walkie Talkie

"That's what we have dry cleaning for!"

At this time, I made my first good decision of the day. I decided to stay out of it and let Fred do it. After all, he had gotten me into this mess; let him clear it up as well. With a big grin, from behind my binoculars, I followed the progress in the boat. After a rather lengthy delay, in which Fred reached an almost complete state of apoplexy, I saw Cornelius, the Security Officer starting to climb the ladder like a giant slug; A yellow tail behind him in the form of a mooring line. The huffs and puffs of the 250-pound ex- marine climbing the vertical ladder, softened after 25 years of good living on cruise ships, were almost audible at 800 feet.

Finally after what looked like an eternity, Cornelius reached the edge of the pier, laboring to get on with the line, which was getting heavier with each step he ascended. Finally he was on the pier and we saw him collapse on his back, still wrapped in the line. Some kindly Mexicans, who had stopped working on their fishing boats to ponder the strange ways of those gringos took it of him and put it on a bollard. The physical work must have taken all of poor Cornelius' energy. I saw him sit down on the dirty dock, amidst crates of fish, not caring at all about his appearance. I could understand how he felt. Heavy black marks left by the dirty mooring line, criss-crossed his shirt like he had been run over by some heavy truck.

"Sir, do you have a minute? The agent is on the radio."

The navigator held his Walkie Talkie up in front of me.

"Yes, this is the Captain, what can I do for you."

"Good morning Captain, just to let you know that the

strike is over. They settled half an hour ago. Didn't want to disturb you, as you were busy. If you want, you can let go your lines, pick up your anchor and come alongside."

We decided to stay where we were. I didn't have the heart to tell Cornelius that his efforts had been in vain. I saw him sitting on the pier for another half hour before he had the energy to get up and walk back on board. His white uniform was never presented to the dry cleaners. The next day, Fred told me with a smirk on his face he had found it in the garbage room.

The Penthouse

The period of being 'Just Married' probably is one of the best times in the life of a man. The delightful curiosity, the realization that after so many years, finally somebody got you, or the other way around, depending from what side one is looking. A home together, making decisions together and sailing together!

We even might have waited a year or so, had it not been for strict company rules, that forbid officers to sail with their friends. Wives on the contrary had almost unlimited privileges of sailing along. We wanted to stay together, so I nervously agreed to take the big plunge into unknown territory. Strangely enough, it was my wife who gave me the final push. Strange, because I had always believed that the male should take the lead in these things. My years on cargo ships must have clouded my sense of reality, when out of pure boredom every book available was read, including the most mushy love stories. In our domestic affairs it soon became clear that Lisa had a mind of her own. Luckily so, as I would never have been interested if she had not.

After a few years of dating, one day, just after I had arrived home, she simply announced that next week we would get married. Unfortunately her timing was a little off, as at that particular moment I had just sat down and taken a deep draught of fresh orange juice, which for the best part of it ended flying over the carpet.

"We will what?"

"We are getting married. I sent out the invitations already, your family is coming over, and it's all arranged."

"My family?" I asked stupidly.

"Yes, it's your mother's idea actually. She told me to arrange it, as it would never occur to you to ask me."

I remember that I found myself refreshing my orange juice, this time adding a generous shot of Vodka to steady my badly shaken nerves. The following week passed in a daze, shopping, sending cards to almost every continent, making calls to faraway friends and of course one telephone call to the company, asking permission for my wife to sail with me during my next contract on board.

The first sign that the head office had received the request was not the permission for my wife to sail, but literally a wave of messages started arriving, congratulating me on my pending marriage. The wave kept coming for quite a while as slowly the news reached the various ships positioned all over the world. My colleagues were as surprised as I had been with my sudden change of status. Most had seen me as the eternal bachelor, a girlfriend every now and then, but always chickening out when the fire became too hot.

The first time to set step on board together we joined the ship in Copenhagen, the beautiful capital of Denmark. It was a gorgeous day in the beginning of August and there hardly could have been a better time to set out on an odyssey through the Baltic, the Mediterranean and the Black sea.

Because of all the hassles of marriage, I had not called our office to find out who else would be on the plane and therefore I was pleasantly surprised to find an old sailing companion sitting in front of me.

The airport at Copenhagen at the height of summer was a mess, tourists, businessmen all were milling around and bumping into each other at the baggage area, anxious for their luggage to arrive. We found ourselves literally amongst thousands of people. The carrousel with our flight number was in the far corner of the terminal, a solid wall of people surrounding it.

"You better try to find a cart, while I stay here to pick the suitcases from the band. They're too heavy for you to pull off from between all those people."

Lisa nodded and disappeared in the crowd. Of course our luggage was the last to arrive and until I had taken it off, I had not given any further thought to my wife. Standing there with a pile of luggage, the size of which suggested more of an expedition into the dark heartlands of Africa, than what was needed for a few months on a cruise ship, I wondered where she was. Suddenly I saw her emerging from the crowds, her blazing eyes not boding any good.

"What took you so long?"

"I found a cart right away, but then some young guy just wrenched it from me. Oh, I'm so mad, I could kill him. I took me 20 minutes to find another one."

With Lisa beside me, still bitterly venting her opinion about the rogue, we loaded the cart and took off, looking for our agent. After a short while we found him talking with our chief engineer, holding a sign with the name of our company. A few others were waiting with him as well, most likely other crew for our ship. I introduced myself to each of them and found out that two of them were new cadets, fresh out of college. Stepping aside to enable them to introduce themselves to my wife, the tallest one suddenly turned white, while Lisa turned a shade redder than she already was.

"That's him, he stole my cart!"

The poor cadet, I could see he almost died then and there. His face flushed from very white to the brightest red I have ever seen. Also the control of his voice was temporarily gone as he uttered sounds which neither I, nor the chief engineer who was standing next to him could understand. From previous sailings, I knew that he was a very bright man, a fact, that enabled him to understand the situation right away. It nearly caused an accident too, as during a terrible burst of laughter erupting from his mouth, he stepped into his suitcases and almost toppled over backward unable to control his movements for the time being. The uncomprehending agent had to steady him, while the whole scene turned into chaos. The apprentice trying to hide behind his much smaller colleague, the agent holding the chief by his arm, my wife talking to me, and I, well I took the side of the chief engineer and started laughing, a fact not very much appreciated by Lisa. Out of the thousands of people on the airport, the poor cadet had to snatch that luggage cart from the captain's wife. A more conspicuous start of his career, I could not imagine.

It took a while before we were ready to get into the mini van the agent had arranged. This time my wife and I did not have to worry about our luggage, the cadets carried it all. Once on board the ship, we quickly settled in our cabin and my wife adopted her role very well. Socializing, talking with guests, escorting tours and in general enjoying herself very much.

"John, I saw on the list that the Penthouse is empty this cruise, isn't that great."

To be honest, I did not immediately see why this was so great. The Penthouse is the most expensive cabin on the ship, right next to mine, with a big balcony and all kinds of luxurious facilities. It being empty meant that the company would not have the revenues from it, and there was nothing good about that. My puzzled expression prompted her to carry on.

"Don't you see, we can use it, I can sit on the balcony and we even can take a bath together in that big Jacuzzi."

My wife is a clever lady, slowly a big smile spread across my face. Why not? The cabin was empty anyway, I had the key and nobody would disturb us. Honesty has me to admit that after thinking about it, I thought it not just a good idea. It plainly was a splendid one, particularly the part about taking the bath together. In fact the tub there is so big that it could prove to be difficult to find each other, once inside it.

We had a formal dinner that evening and decided that afterward we would carry out the plan and enjoy ourselves. Of course there are also Jacuzzis on the public decks, but somehow I always have found it a little awkward to sit in a tub with complete strangers coming and going. It's almost like taking a shower in public. Maybe it's because I grew up in a prudish family where nudity was regarded as allright, provided it was in a bathroom with the latch on the door.

Around 9 p.m. that evening, I opened the door of the huge cabin. We first sat on the balcony for a while. I remembered that the place was equipped with a mini bar and decided to have a look if there was anything to my liking. A Glenfiddich would be quite acceptable, I thought humbly, and poured myself a stiff one, while Lisa made herself a Bloody Mary.

After enjoying the evening for a little while I decided to start running the water in the tub. This would take some time and I returned to the balcony and Lisa, to quietly watch the stars and the ocean. The peace and tranquility of the immense seas always had a powerful effect on me. Sometimes I regret not being a watch-keeping officer anymore, doing the dog shift in the middle of the night and feeling only too happy to work during these very lonely hours. It is very difficult to describe the feelings of being on the bridge of a ship at night. Being the King on God's oceans maybe comes close. Sitting there on that balcony I considered myself the most fortunate man in the world.

Startled I woke up from my dreaming; the water was running after all. Time to check it. The tub was a little over half full and I called Lisa to get in. I threw my uniform on the bed and my shoes went somewhere else in the cabin. I would find them later. Lisa did the same and a few minutes later we were up to our necks in the water, while I switched on the pumps. Feeling totally satisfied with the world, I sipped my second Glenfiddich and let myself float, bodily as well as mentally.

We must have sat there for at least an hour when Lisa announced she was getting out, after all it was almost 11 p.m., time to go to our own cabin and to bed. Sleepily I watched her picking up a towel, not minding if it would take her awhile, as I was still happily submerged. From the corner of my eyes I saw her looking around the marble bathroom, in awe with all the luxury. She opened a cupboard to look inside.

"Hans, I'm so amazed about all this. It has everything; bathrobes, hairdryers, a   shaver..."

"Yea, I wish we could afford something like it...What did you say, a shaver, we don't provide shavers!"

A sudden sinking feeling in my stomach warned of looming disaster.

"Quick, look in the other cabinets."

Not suspecting anything yet, Lisa opened the closest closet and I saw her hand moving in front of her mouth.

"Hans, there are clothes, lots of them, also in the drawers, Oh my God."

Simultaneously we reached the same conclusion. The cabin was not empty. Like a breaching whale, I rose from the water, painfully hitting my knee against the faucet without even noticing it at first.

"Let's get out of here, fast!"

I grabbed the first towel I could find and desperately tried to retrieve the various parts of my uniform, deeply regretting the fact that I had thrown them about so haphazardly. Lisa was doing the same with her cloths and with equal urgency. Dressed in a towel and loaded with belongings, I carefully opened the cabin door and peeked outside. There was nobody in the corridor. As fast as we could we dashed out, around the corner and into my cabin, which thank goodness I had not locked. Still dripping wet I sat down and shakily picked up the phone.

"Front desk, can I help you?"

"Captain here, can you tell me if the Penthouse is occupied?"

"Let me look… yes sir, we sold it this afternoon to a couple from New York."

Without bothering any further I slammed down the phone.

"House keeping, good evening."

"Captain here, I need three stewards, on the double, let them go to the Penthouse and clean up the bathroom, dirty glasses and just everything else that is not as it should be, fast!"

Hurriedly I got dressed and started peeping around the corner at the sudden activity in the Penthouse. Stewards were walking in and out with towels, and dirty glasses. Thank God for an experienced crew. It all took not more than ten minutes and I exhaled a deep sigh of relief when I saw the last steward leave.

"They're finished." I whispered to Lisa who was standing behind me also fully dressed now. Just when I wanted to close the door, I heard a voice and looked again. A nice couple was standing at the door outside the Penthouse, the man fumbling for the key while she hugged him. Finally I could safely close the door and when I looked at Lisa we both started to laugh uncontrollably. The thought of the couple coming back in their expensive cabin and at first finding clothes all over the cabin, including the Captain's uniform and finally finding the Captain and his wife in their bath was just too much.

Ever since this happened, I have still used the Penthouse occasionally, but never before checking if it is sold or not. Even then, when inside, I double lock the door, just to be safe.

The Duck Died

When one has sailed on cruise ships for many years, somewhere there is a point of no return; A point where you decide, whether this is the type of life for you or not. For some this is after a few weeks and for others it takes years. One of the main reasons why after a few years I decided to stay was that I felt a sense of being part of a family and belonging. It starts when a few, initially superficial, friendships become stronger and in some cases bond into lifetime relations. The fact, that in the earlier days, the companies were a lot smaller than today also attributed to my decision. You sail more often with the people you know, and nobody on board is a real stranger anymore.

At first the crew becomes more and more familiar, and later on the passengers. Often it happens that passengers plan their vacations according to their crewmember friend's schedule. This last phenomena, is certainly not limited to the officers. Virtually every crewmember, who has been at sea for a while, knows guests who come back only to meet him or her. In such circumstances, over the years it becomes more and more difficult to quit sailing. In this rather unconventional mix of relations, at least from an outsider's point of view, there is one group standing out even more. They are a colorful assembly of individuals, unceremoniously called 'Entertainment'. Many of them stay away from other crewmembers, their worlds being so far apart. On the other hand, I also often have witnessed that the groups reached out to each other and did so for the better of the whole ship. However, there is one sad fact, common to the majority of the Entertainers. After one term on a ship, they usually disappear and we never see them back.

None of them? No, not all disappear into the gray mass of humanity ashore, some do come back, liking the lifestyle and enjoying the friendships made. A few are my longtime friends. Excellent artists, delivering quality shows, making the audience laugh, exclaim or sit in awe, all depending on their particular expertise.

When John Reeves knocked on my door, it was a meeting again after at least four years. He had been on other ships and had taken some time off to produce a new show, he told me. This did amaze me and worried me at the same time. John's shows were always the same, almost to the letter. Still they never failed to make me laugh so much that invariably my stomach ached at the end of the evening. A new show would be difficult to imagine after ten years of the same. There even was a chance that the passengers, who also knew him, would not like all that new nonsense. They might want to hear the same old jokes, laughing and anticipating the exact lines he would use.

The next evening was a very busy one for me, but nevertheless I decided to go to the show. I wanted to hear if it was as good as the old one and hopefully John would not disappoint me.

Well, John was a professional and knew what he was doing. He had not taken any risks and apart from a few minor new twists, his 'new' show was exactly the same as the old one. The audience, many of who had sailed with us many times before and who also knew John, loved it and so did I. For an hour forgotten were all the daily worries and concerns a captain has and I laughed about his jokes as before.

One of his jokes, predictable to the minute like all others, was about his small hometown, so small that they had to close down the zoo, when the duck died. When reading this, it does not sound too funny at all, but John was a master storyteller and the audience roared with laughter.

A few days later, during a coffee break, one of the Navigation Officers mentioned John and his old jokes.

"Wouldn't it be fun to try a joke on him while he is on stage, he is so predictable."

When people have a common goal of fooling a fellow man, there is no limit as to what they will do to pull it off. Maybe I should have interfered, but on the other hand, what is better than an innocent joke. A joke that everybody, including the victim, can laugh about. The officers were discussing how to pull something off and at the same time keep it clean, when all of a sudden the Security Officer, a devious man to say the least, raised his hand.

"I got it, listen."

Slowly during his explanation, I saw all faces starting to grin, mine too. This promised to be good.

At that time we were doing weekly cruises in beautiful Alaska and during one of our weekly calls at Sitka, when strolling around town, he had seen a pond with several ducks. Would it not be a great idea to catch one and set it loose on stage during the show, right after John had told the audience that the duck had died in his local zoo. I decided that whilst knowing of the general plan, it would be better for me not to know too much. Captains are supposed to be a little more serious than to involve themselves in practical jokes.

The few days preceding our call in Sitka, the officers were in a funny mood, giggling and joking with each other all the time. I always have believed that when jokes are being played on board a ship, a captain has less to worry about, as the atmosphere is good then. Planning this joke surely did boost morale and by the time we reached Sitka the whole crew knew about it, except of course poor John. Had he been more observant and less trusting, he would have guessed that something was bound to happen, as every crew he met smiled at him. John with his always-good mood didn't think about it twice and only returned the smiles.

Capturing the duck turned out to be a story in itself, one of which I was the only witness. Daniel, our security officer had contacted our agent and obtained permission to catch a duck, provided the animal would be returned unharmed. Reluctantly I had given permission to keep the duck on board for a week, even though it is against regulations to keep animals on the ship. She would be returned to her Sitka pond during the following cruise. Our bosun had provided Daniel with a net of the type fisherman use to retrieve fish, only twice as big. The end of it, he had attached to an extension pole used by the sailors to paint difficult to reach far away spots. His equipment was complemented with a bag full of stale croissants given to him by the Baker. Croissants, Daniel swore were a duck's most coveted delicacy. Adjusting his glasses, he left the ship by tender and I decided to follow him.

Ashore, our agent was waiting for him and together they took off to the other side of town where a couple of ducks were rumored to be in a pond. Taking my seat on a park bench, I saw them not too far away. Daniel dubiously was looking at a small boat, as if weighing his chances of survival in such a small unstable craft. You have to know that he had been with us for more years than I can remember and the good life on cruise ship had not been too physically taxing for him. I could almost taste his apprehension and his feeling that he should have looked up the word 'exercise' a little more in his dictionary. Finally he got in and precariously balancing the little craft, he pushed off to the middle of the pond.

"Poule poule poule!"

I chuckled. Daniel, we all knew had grown up in France

and was calling the ducks in his native tongue. I don't think it made a lot of difference to the ducks, watching him from a safe distance, but here in Sitka it sounded decidedly strange to me.

"To your right, Daniel!"

The girl called. He turned around and with the net made a wild movement, which if it did not catch the duck that had swam a little closer to the boat to satisfy his curiosity with this strange human being, it certainly would give the poor animal a near heart attack. As it turned out, it was the first of the two possibilities.

This amazed me, catching a duck was far simpler than I had thought and I resolved not to forget this, being a great lover of poultry, and knowing that not too far from my house are several ponds.

The duck, a big fat animal, used to lazing his, (or her, I'm not sure of this) days away, waiting to be fed by the elderly occupants of a nearby retirement home, did not appreciate being caught in a net. Through the mazes he snapped at Daniel, making him almost fall overboard twice, while he tried to put the bird in a cardboard box. The duck was not the cleanest one I've ever seen either and during Daniel's desperate attempts to subdue him, he lavishly sprayed him with material, which my publisher asked me to call dirt.

It took a while before Daniel managed to get back ashore. He walked back to the tender with the box under his arms when I joined him.

"We can keep him in cabin 1012, it's empty, I already checked with the Purser, I better take good care of him, look what he did."

He showed me two bruises on his hand and arm where the duck had bitten him.

While talking to him, it became obvious that Daniel, like

me, had not the vaguest idea of how to determine the gender of a duck, understandably of course, as the ability to do so, until now, had not mattered the slightest in our professional careers.

"What do you mean cabin 1012!"

"Well, we have to keep her somewhere and 1012 has a bathtub…I thought…"

He didn't continue; we had reached the tender, leaving me dumbfounded. A real cabin for a duck? I couldn't really back out anymore, being too far involved, and we had promised to treat the duck well. In the end everybody was happy, including, I believe, the duck that settled well in his cabin deluxe, with the tub doubling up as an artificial pond.

I felt a little sorry for poor John that evening. A few times during his performance I saw him looking up at the balcony, surprised at the enormous number of officers and crew who had come to see his show. Even amongst the guests there was a mood of anticipation as some crew members on the lookout for a higher tip at the end of the cruise has obligingly filled them in on the coming event.

"I live in a town so small, that one day we had to close the zoo. You know why…. because the duck died!"

Used to a certain amount of mirth when telling this joke, John was totally unprepared for the roaring laughter from the audience. With his back to the stage, he did not see what was happening behind him. Had he told the joke differently? That would explain the reaction of the public, because if so, he had to remember to do it again.

In the mean time the duck paraded back and forth over the stage. Had we rehearsed ten times, it would not have gone any better. Suddenly the duck spotted a few elderly ladies in the front row. These were the type of persons who always fed him in his pond. He headed straight for them, focusing primarily on their purses, which surely were filled with morsels of bread.

"Quack quack!"

John jumped almost three feet high.

"Quack quack quack."

He had been on stage all his life and chose the wisest way out and joined the fun. Continuing his show he regularly burst out laughing and we all joined him as a better show we hadn't seen yet.

Seldom was a joke on board a ship more successful as that time with the duck. Even now after more than ten years some of the returning passengers still talk about it. The duck was returned to her pond in Sitka, a celebrity amongst other ducks for sure, being the only one of her breed to have completed an Alaska cruise.

Unknown to us at that time was the fact that Daniel played his own little trick on our agent. Having had to make several pledges to return the duck unharmed, he arrived at the pier with the first tender, looking very distraught and guilty. Without saying much, he handed her the box with the duck inside, which she carefully opened to have a peek. Inside she found a whole fried duck, its legs sticking up. The girls almost started to cry but then she heard, "Quack quack...." The duck did not like being left alone in the tender and had sat in the entrance looking around. The girl did shed some tears, but now from laughter, and pulled Daniel's cap over his eyes.

This was the end of the duck story, as jokes are only funny when there is an end to them, or was it? It would have been, had our House Keeping Department not forgotten to clean up the cabin the duck had occupied.

We had arrived back in Vancouver and Ron Sherwin, another entertainer; one of those proven men, sure to be a success with his audience had joined the ship. As usual he was assigned a cabin...within minutes he was back at Guest Services, rather upset.

"My cabin is dirty as a pigsty, the bathroom smells, feathers all over. I won't go in, you have to clean it first."

A few days later, I overheard a conversation between Ron and one of his colleagues. They were comparing their cabins.

"I have a real nice cabin, clean, spacious, nothing to complain about, what about yours?"

Disgust appeared on Ron's face. "My cabin? You want to know about my cabin? Last cruise the company rented it out to a bloody duck!"

The Evacuation

Looking down upon the dock at the line of embarking passengers, I could only be relieved that I had them back on board. Our stop at the little Spanish port of Vigo was only scheduled so we could pick up an overland tour, that had left the ship earlier that day in La Coruna. During all my years as a captain, I've never felt comfortable leaving a harbor with only half the passengers on board, while the other half were traveling by bus or train to the next port. It must be the same for every captain, the knowledge that when something happens there is very little one can do. On board ship we can take action, your own trustworthy crew immediately available.

Very content I leaned in the windowsill, seeing the line of people getting shorter, only a few hundred to go. Turning around I saw the ship's agent, patiently waiting, with a stack of papers to be signed. With a sigh I left my half finished cup of coffee and liberally started putting my signature on an amazing amount of forms.

It has never stopped to amaze me, how many people are interested in the signature of a captain. Port fees, six copies, agency fees, four copies, the water bill, four copies, and on it went. Every now and then I have bad dreams when suddenly the company decides to hold me responsible for every bill I signed without double-checking it. Usually it ends with me waking up, resolving once and for all, never to sign them anymore without going over them at least three times. But then, the next port is in Russia and you are handed a stack of paper a foot high, 20 minutes before departure. Need less to say, that by now I'm resigned to having a bad dream every now and then.

"Everybody on board sir, and the engine room is ready for departure."

Saying good-bye to the agent, the big smile on his face when he looked at the signed papers, made me dread the coming night.

I can truly say that the open sea, the far horizons and the endless skies, make a person feel different, less restricted. Often in the evenings, I just stand on a deserted deck, staring into the dark night, and it is amazing how much there is to see. Even more amazing to me is how few of the guests on board can be found on deck at this time. During the day everybody is out, sitting in the sun, lazing the day away. They sip on exotic cocktails, often an undrinkable concoction, thought up by the barkeeper himself, but agreed by all who know him, to be the best they ever tasted. At night, the ship's life continues inside, leaving the decks to the few who want to be alone. I was standing on the top deck, utterly content, looking at the distant stars.

A deck below me, a young couple did the same and a few things more. They had not seen me and of course I did not disturb them. It could not have been more than 10 minutes before my time of solitude was invaded by modern technology. Nowadays most people want to be reachable no matter where they are, and a captain of a cruise ship is no exception. My beeper went off, rudely pulling me back into reality. While to me this was a common event, the couple standing only a few yards away had no clue where this sound came from. While stepping back where they could not see me, I could hear her yelp and then a sound like somebody was slapped in the face. It made me smile; at least I was not the only one whose quiet evening was being disturbed.

"The hospital called sir, they have an emergency. The doctor asked me to call you."

A medical emergency always comes unexpected. Often late at night making us wonder why people cannot come to the infirmary at normal hours. I think that every physician has had this same experience many times over. To be honest, I do not mind being called as long as I'm not asleep yet.

"She is 61 years old and bleeding internally."

Sailing together for many years, Dr. Sandberg by now knew not to bother me with terms too medical, as he invariably would be asked to explain in a way more understandable for a commoner. Every navigation officer in our company received a rather comprehensive training to the extent of working in a hospital for a minimum of three months so we should be able to understand some of the jargon. However after misunderstanding my medical staff a few times and subsequently making a fool of myself, I prefer the easier explanation.

"How bad is it?"

A long silence on the other side of the line made me fear the worst.

"I'm not 100% sure, but I believe that we can't do very much; it looks bad."

Another silence followed during which I heard some voices murmuring.

"Four hours at the most."

"Are you sure?"

This was of course a silly question. Sandberg was a very competent doctor, who had saved many lives during his years on ships. He certainly knew what he was talking about. Four hours, my God, that did not give us much time to take action. I looked at the clock, eleven p.m., without looking at the map I knew we were just about half way between Vigo and our next port, Lisbon.

Feverishly we calculated, the navigation officer, a bleary-eyed staff captain, who unlike me, had been asleep, and myself, checking maps of the empty Portuguese coast. Going back to Vigo or continuing to Lisbon, both were no options, both hours beyond the four given to us. When looking at the maps I started to wish this were the American coast, where there is always the blessed presence of the Coast Guard. Many a passenger and as a matter of fact, numerous crew members as well, owe their lives to this organization which is always there and ready to help. How in the world would I be able to get a helicopter to the ship, here 45 miles away from any shore? The navigator kept leafing through his maps. Suddenly I had an idea.

"Try and look up Leixoes."

"Leixoes?"

I remembered that many years ago, during a trip on a cargo ship, on our way from Japan to Europe, we had stopped at this little place. It couldn't be too far away from our present position!

"Too small, we never could get in."

The navigator said, when he had found it.

"We don't have to, maybe they can send a boat so we can transfer her. Call the engine room to go to emergency speed and give me a course for Leixoes."

Back in my office I tried to get in touch with the Portuguese Coast Guard, and very soon I found out that this was no easy task. Yes, I got through to them soon enough, but trying to tell them what exactly our problem was proved to be beyond my lingual capabilities. Leixoes, according to the books, a small port visited by medium sized cargo ships, clearly was not high on the priority list of the Portuguese Coast Guard to put English-speaking personnel on duty. Now what? Maybe I could contact our agent in Lisbon, who then in turn could alert the authorities in Leixoes. Hurriedly I went through the company's agent book. Le Havre, Leith, Leixoes, Lisbon.... Suddenly I realized that the previous page had said 'Leixoes'. I turned back and yes it was unbelievable but true. We had an agent listed in Leixoes.

How often had I criticized our company for not updating some of their books? Never would I do this again, the slackness of some anonymous office soul, might save a life today. When I called the agent he needed a considerable amount of time to figure out who was calling and what was going on. After all it must have been 20 years since he last had anything to do with our company. Then suddenly being called out of his first sleep, forced to speak English over a not too good a connection, was a little more than his brain would take at first. After a slow start he suddenly seemed to jump into a higher gear however.

How grateful I was that all this was happening close to Portugal. Of all the peoples in Southern Europe, the Portuguese probably have the best understanding and the most efficient ways of handling emergencies at sea. Centuries of seafaring and exploring the world, definitely has left this country with an admirable legacy. Once Mr. Rawes had climbed out of his bed, things started rolling.

I looked at the wall clock and rubbed my face. Twelve thirty and we had at least an hour and a half to go before we would reach the coast. I prayed that there would be no delays and that everything would be ready once we arrived. We would have only one hour to stop the ship, transfer the patient ashore by boat, get her to the hospital and get a blood transfusion started. To say that it didn't look good at all would be an understatement. The telephone rang.

"We are in touch with the pilot station sir."

"I'll be up in a second."

Running to the bridge, I could only hope that all would be

going well.

"Leixoes pilot this is the Captain speaking."

Immediately the pilot came back on the radio, telling me that the port was closed because of dense fog, we had to stay out. Expecting that this complication would slow everything down and cause a deadly delay, I started to figure out what to do now. A minute later the pilot station came back and told me what to do.

"We need you to lower a boat of your own, our pilot boat can't take stretchers. She is too small. We will send her out however so she can guide your boat into the harbor."

Thank God for those sensible people. They provided me with a solution without the need of lengthy discussions.

"Call out the bosun and four sailors, a deck officer and an engineer. Tell them to make a tender ready as soon as possible."

In more normal conditions, the tenders are used to ferry passengers ashore in ports too small for the ship to enter. We carried four of them. They resembled very much a floating bus, with rows of seats on each side. Fast little boats, and thanks to whoever designed them, equipped with radar.

Quickly the crew reporting for emergency duties started to appear on the bridge, an officer to pick up check lists, the bosun for portable radios and the security officer to report that all the personal belongings of the patient had been packed and were ready to be put in the tender.

By now we could see the outline of the port of Leixoes on the radar, still half an hour away. We were still going on our top speed and it was about time to start slowing down. It wouldn't do us any good, speeding by a waiting pilot boat, not being able to stop in time, leaving them wondering what the idea was. The fog slowly was thickening and outside it looked like a thick gray blanket had been lowered over the ship, making me a little uncomfortable sailing this fast so close to the coast.

"We have the patient on deck at the tender. As soon as you give us the go ahead we can embark her and her husband and lower the tender."

Daniel, our security officer had done similar exercises many times before and sounded as calm as could be. In the many times I sailed with him, during emergencies, he was always confident, knowing that it was the only way to make an operation go smoothly.

Lowering the tender took only a few moments and via the radio I could follow what was happening. On the radar we saw a dot coming closer, but from the bridge, high above the water we could not see the pilot boat. After they made contact with our tender, we could follow their progress on the radar. Painfully slow they approached the breakwater and then disappeared into the harbor. It was two thirty.

"I can see an ambulance on the pier, we will be there in 5 minutes." Daniel reported. It seemed like an eternity before the next message came through,

"We are transferring the patient into the ambulance, there are a lot of people to help."

"We are on our way back to the ship."

Shortly afterward on the radar screen I could see a little dot appearing from behind the breakwater of Leixoes harbor.

Yawning I stood on the bridge, a few too short hours later, welcoming the Lisbon pilot on board. With some regret I realized that the sightseeing in the city, that I had planned for this afternoon would have to be cancelled. Because of all the hassle, we were arriving two hours late, and this probably would mean a lot of extra paperwork and some of our guests would have to be pacified about missing their tour. On top of this, I needed to catch up on my sleep.

Arriving in Lisbon by ship always is spectacular, the wide

river with all kinds of traffic, the hanging bridge, high enough to allow even the biggest ship to sail through, and above all, the city. I always looked at this place in awe. From here the world was explored and discovered. From here Vasco da Gama and Bartholomew Diaz left and returned, telling a still medieval world about the wonders they had seen. In Belem Tower, Prince Henry the Seafarer sat, watching his ships sail, to conquer and to found one of the world's greatest empires. Lisbon is submerged in history, making one feel it almost can be touched.

Docking a ship in this port is often a tricky business. The current on the river frequently is treacherous and strong and at unexpected times pushes a ship towards the dock too fast, or it acts like a cushion making the process very slow. Even thinking about docking in Lisbon could accelerate the heartbeat of a Captain by a solid 100%.

The Portuguese pilots are the closest descendants of men like Da Gama and know what it is to be a Captain and give their advice to the best of their knowledge, which is considerable. The pilot coming on board that morning without question had some of the blood of his great ancestors in his veins. Over the many centuries since, in his particular case however, it must have been diluted with a large amount of blood, which seemed better suited to fill the veins of a stuntman in Hollywood. The advice he supplied me with, came in short bursts of speech, which took some time to understand and after I had figured out what he was saying, I was mostly glad that in the mean time I already had done the opposite. The pilot did not seem to mind that his advice was not followed up to the letter and he smiled at me happily with his mouth open, each time parting with an overpowering odor of decaying garlic.

So, somewhat distracted, I think it perfectly understandable that I did not immediately understand what the agent was talking about when he came on board.

"She's doing fine."

After he repeated himself, it dawned on me that he was talking about the woman we had evacuated the previous night.

"Tell me all about her!"

"Well I was on the phone with the doctor just half an hour ago and she made it. Had you been 15 minutes later he said, it would have been too late. She will be out of the hospital in a few days and fly home to the U.S."

My spirits lifted and all fatigue seemed to fall away from me. We had saved a life, something, that does not happen everyday and I felt genuinely proud. I decided to go sightseeing after all. Didn't I deserve to treat myself? Humming I went to my cabin to have breakfast.

It was about a week later, after embarking new passengers we had continued into the Mediterranean. Everybody on board, passengers, crew and certainly the captain were in the best of spirits. All was going well, beautiful weather, a good group on board and an excellent itinerary. The chief engineer and I were sitting together having a glass of wine, when again my beeper went off. Knowing it could not be about technical problems, as surely they would have beeped the chief engineer first, I dialed in.

"Yes Captain, this is the Radio Officer, there is an urgent call for you from head office, if you could call them back as soon as possible."

Urgent calls from head office in my experience are not always too urgent. I can remember not too long ago that I urgently had to call the vice president himself. I had left an excellent dinner and a very enjoyable group of passengers to make the call.

"Good evening, I had to call you urgently."

"Uh...what?"

"I received a message to call you."

"Oh yes, let me think what was it again...Oh yes, next time you are in port, could you send me two kilos of French cheese, we are having a party in a few weeks."

I returned to the chief engineer to finish my wine, when ten minutes later my beeper went of again. This time it was the staff captain, telling me to call head office without delay. The wine was finished anyway and maybe this time it was truly urgent.

"What did you do to Mrs. Ronley?"

"Mrs. Who?"

At that moment I honestly did not immediately remembmr the name of the woman we evacuated. I was at a loss of what to think about the abrupt manners of the Director Risk Management on the other side of the line.

"Mrs. Ronley, you evacuated her and her husband off the ship a week ago in Portugal."

"What we did to her? Nothing, we got her to a hospital in the middle of the night, that's all."

I told him what had happened, in the mean time becoming very curious about the reason for this call.

"They are suing us, saying that you put them through a harrowing experience. Put them in a small boat and dropped them in a foreign country without help. She could have died there, they claim."

"What! She would have died for sure had we left them on board."

For the next half hour, I recounted exactly what we had done and why. As for myself, I felt drained and tired. Instead of getting a thank you, I was looking forward to a lawsuit.

Even looking back, now that many years have passed, I still get a sad feeling about this. For three years in a row, I was reminded of Mrs. Ronley when during my vacations I had to travel to the United States to make sworn dispositions and appear in court twice. In the end I guess justice prevailed when the case was dismissed. They did not get any money out of it and neither did I; the only thing it cost me was a year or so of my life. Maybe I will sue her for this.

Terrorists

Terrorists, the very word sends shivers through my spine and most likely that of every normal person in the world.

Partnering with the various ports, the cruise lines have gradually stepped up their security measures and are regularly audited to see how well they are doing. Gone are the days that virtually anyone could walk on board almost unchallenged. Nowadays visitors have to be announced days before the cruise starts and have to be approved and re-approved.

Gone with the easier attitude, are also the farewell parties where family and friends came on board with bottles of champagne and trays of snacks. During those few hours before departure, it could happen that at times, there were two times as many people on board, than actually had booked for the cruise. I still believe that it is a miracle that we did not have more stowaways in those days than we did.

Modern ships are equipped with all kinds of gadgets, most of which I only vaguely understand. Passengers are screened, luggage is X-rayed and checked and above all the crew is alert and knows what to look for.

Occasionally this alertness gives reason for alarm, which, thank God, so far all have been false. The worst scare we had, and at the same time the most hilarious, occurred on a sunny day in Vancouver, many years ago. Security systems were less sophisticated and an alert crewmember at the gangway usually was the only person who was seriously checking those coming on board the ship.

We had started to embark the passengers for our next

cruise to Alaska. I was in an excellent mood; the previous cruise had been a success with happy guests and the weather for the coming week looked promising too. It must be the same for every person, that when all goes smooth and the prospects are bright, one starts to wonder if maybe something will go wrong soon, or is wrong already. Without any good reason, I had this sinking feeling in my stomach when I picked up the phone.

"Could you please come to the bridge sir, we have a slight problem."

How often had I heard a similar voice before, never telling me that everything was going fine, always 'a slight problem'. Throwing the book I was reading in a corner, I ran upstairs.

"What's the matter?"

"Could you call the Security Officer at the gangway, sir."

On this particular cruise, I had the pleasure of sailing again with Daniel, a seemingly slow, but in reality a very sharp man. Hiding under a layer of 'Gentleman' veneer and thick glasses, was the mind of a German Shepard. I knew that all security matters were in safe hands with him.

"What's the matter, Daniel?"

The worried sound of his voice made me expect the worst and it proved to be right.

"Don't know what to think about, but we seem to have an awful lot of passengers coming on board, who are from the Middle East. You know that every now and then we have a few from Egypt or Lebanon, but never more than five or six."

"What do you mean, how many are there this time? No better come to the bridge.

I'll send somebody down to cover for you for a few minutes."

He told me that while at first not noticing anything unusual, it had suddenly hit him that after seeing the first two or three hundred tickets and passports, there seemed to be an abnormal amount of passports from Tunisia being presented to him.

"You know, they are still coming in as I speak. They don't come in together either, like a family would. I did a quick sweep of the public rooms and I found some of them sitting together in the library. They also talked with some people who checked in on other passports, Canadian and American ones."

I didn't see the blue skies and the warm sun anymore as clouds had started to gather at least they did so in my mind.

"What are their names and what do they look like? Do you think they are a group?"

"Well, I don't really know what the names of terrorists are supposed to be like, but to me it all looks a little suspicious."

Terrorists, mentioning the word unthinkingly, Daniel had no idea how much he unsettled me. I tried to collect my thoughts. This was no joke and that too on my ship! We decided to do a quick walk through the ship, while the Purser who I had alerted was going through the passenger manifest to check the names Daniel had collected, to compare their cabin numbers with their nationality.

"Look, that's one of them and there, another one. Look, he starts talking with that one over there."

I followed Daniels's direction and indeed saw a few men nodding to others at the other side of the room. To say that I was a little nervous would be the understatement of the year. The two men at the other side of the room, looked like the perfect villains to me. Heavy moustaches, unshaven, crumpled cloths. Yes, definitely a pair who, in my imagination fitted the picture perfectly. My blood started boiling.

"Maybe I better call head office, they should be able to give me some input about what to do."

The answer I got was not very satisfactory at all.

"What! Oh no, what are you going to do?"

"I don't know; I had hoped you could give me some more information."

"Me? What makes you think that? You are the captain, you decide what to do."

A reminder about me being the captain was not really what I needed, as that fact had been on my mind ever since the security officer had called me with his suspicions. Even though my mind was in turmoil, I did get some satisfaction, hearing Peter stutter in the phone, all the way from Miami. Is there not a saying after all that shared misery is half misery? After battling on the phone for a few minutes, Peter came up with a good idea.

"Give me a list with the names you have and we will run them through our computers, see if somehow there is a connection with others and if there's anything wrong."

I put the phone down and when I looked in the mirror opposite me, I saw that the little bit color, so carefully built up during a few hours I had to spend out on the bridge wings each week, had completely left my face. Daniel walked in without even bothering to knock, indicating that he too was somewhat out of his normal behavior. He had some more names to add to our list and we started to compare them again. The telephone rang and I snatched it.

"Yes."

"Peter here, yes, you were right, there is something wrong here. We ran the names you gave us and at first found nothing, but we did it again, comparing them with other names and checked their travel agent. They all booked through the same agent in New York, also found quite a few not on your list."

"So, what did that agent tell you when you called them,

are they normal passengers or not?"

"Well, that is to say, we tried to find their telephone number, but there was none. We found out that everything was paid through some credit card issued by a bank in Bahrain in the name of some Lebanese family. The travel agency doesn't even exist."

Open mouthed I gaped at Daniel who listening through the speaker phone. My mind was not working, as it should be.

"How many names?" I managed to croak.

"Forty seven, most of them men, about ten single women, a few older than fifty. Looks like you have some trouble on your hands."

Daniel paled, and with a furtive glance behind him, he looked as if he was ready to bolt for the door and leave me with the problem.

"We better get some help from the Canadian Authorities; we can't handle something like this."

Trying to look inconspicuous and pretending to be engrossed in normal business we headed for the gangway. Some of the guests cast some questioning glances at us. A white-faced captain followed by a security officer close to tears and with fogging glasses does provoke the suspicion that something is amiss.

Once outside, the first person we met was our agent who, after initially ruining his seven hundred dollar radio, which he dropped on the marble floor of the terminal, started to make phone calls. Until that day I never realized how efficient Special Forces could be. I know that everybody, when reading books about all kinds of impossible actions does take this with a certain grain of salt, well I can tell you, reality is just as good.

First I have to say that I never knew exactly what people they sent us. I call them 'Special Forces' as they were unbelievingly effective. Within ten minutes a young gentleman in a gray three piece suit, who looked very much like Arnold Schwarzenegger, knocked on my door.

"Good day sir, you are the Captain?"

It was more a statement than a question.

"The boys are coming on board and we need your help to point out the suspects to us. Maybe we should walk through the ship with your people. I understand we know their cabin numbers, so we can check those out first. Do we have a room where we can separate them from the other passengers?"

I told them that the Purser, Daniel and me would go with them. Immediately after having said this, the realization dawned on me that this could be dangerous. Bullets could be flying around and in such an environment I would be the only untrained person. My bladder suddenly manifested itself and I told the guy I would be with him in a minute.

Alone in the bathroom I looked in the mirror and tried look menacing, but with very little success. The angry look of a cruise ship Captain surely would not intimidate a terrorist planning to take over his ship.Ducking, that was the better thing to do and while pretending to wash my hands, I let myself fall of the floor to see how fast this could be done. Falling was certainly not slow, neither was hitting my head against the sink, but again, it was a far cry from being convincing.

We assembled on the bridge, six groups; Three to go through the cabins and the other three doing the public rooms. The latter accompanied by the Security Officer, the Purser and me. None of us looked too happy about the prospect of possibly having to confront men as dangerous as terrorists. Looking out of a window, I saw Vancouver. The place looked like paradise to me. If only I was walking the streets as a bookkeeper or collecting garbage, anything but being a cruise ship Captain.

"Let's go."

Unsuccessfully trying to put a smile on my face, we walked

through the Main Lounge looking around; I hesitated,

"You see them?"

"O...over t..there."

"Walk over and pretend you are showing us something."

"W..well, this is the st..stage, that's where the sh..show is every night."

We approached the two men, the same ones who earlier had fitted so perfectly in the picture as being terrorists. They did not seem to notice us, but that of course was a fake. A terrorist, I knew, was always aware of the people around him. All of a sudden the two men disappeared and amazed I looked behind me. They were both lying on the floor spread-eagled. My spirits soared tenfold.

"Bring them to the meeting room, the scum!"

After all, in difficult situations I know what to do. Arriving in the room, I saw that we were the last ones to bring in our prisoners. The others were sitting along the walls, manacled and carefully covered by the Canadians. Daniel had completely regained his composure and behaved with a rather cocky attitude, rather much reversed from what I had seen earlier.

Nobody said anything; all eyes were directed at me. I looked around and focused on what looked like a terrorist in his early seventies, who must be the leader.

"You, what are you doing here?"

I asked in a harsh voice. One never should be too easy going with low lives like that, specially not when they are captured. The man looked at me.

"I thought to take a cruise to Alaska." He said.

Expecting a lie, I never thought it possible for them to be stupid enough to believe I would go for such an answer.

"Come on, tell me the truth, you are a group, mostly from the Middle East and you know each other."

"Yes, of course we know each other, we are all family. We

organized this cruise as a reunion."

I was ready to make a sneering remark, but something inside me warned me not to. I saw that the old man actually looked too dignified to fit my picture and that the others didn't look like captured criminals either.

"But what about that non existing travel agent in New York? I bet you don't have an answer for that."

A smile suddenly started to form on his lips and some of the other captives even started to laugh, steadying themselves with their manacled hands.

"You!"

The old man roared at a younger guy in a corner who made futile attempts to look unconcerned.

"It's all your fault. You and your special group discount provided you could pretend being a travel agent. Well, you did alright, two free cabins and all of us arrested!"

"You mean..."

"Yes, we are on a family reunion, it's organized by my younger son, that one over there, who decided to cut some corners."

Relief and embarrassment contended for precedence inside me. The Canadians collapsed on the floor, screaming with fun and even the still manacled terrorists saw the humor of the situation. I was immensely happy that they took it as a good joke. Something they would without doubt, talk about for years. During the cruise that followed we did everything we could for this, by now, very special group. Nothing was too much and we became friends. Sometimes I still see some of them cruising with us, and each time, we share an understanding smile.

The Takeover

There are often days, which when one looks back, he wishes he would not have gotten out of bed that morning. Days doomed right from the start. It was on one of those days. It started when the telephone on my desk rang early that morning, waking me up. Of course, it's only a manner of speaking, as a captain cannot really afford not to answer his telephone or not to get out of bed. But still, when looking back, it was a day I would rather forget. Of course, I was having no such thoughts at the time, when unsuspectingly I picked up the receiver:

"Hans, it's Peter here, there have been some things happening that I have to fill you in about."

A voice, I recognized as belonging to a friend of me, said.

My brain, not yet having cleared the mists of a heavy sleep, failed to immediately register the urgency in his voice. I sat up, propped a pillow behind my back, and looked at the alarm clock. It showed 4 am.

"Do you know what time it is over here? Have you forgotten that there are time-zones in the world?"

Peter, my long time pal, had chosen a career ashore many years before and was now running the operations department of our company. We had known each other from our early days at the nautical college and we even had joined the same cargo company. Then we had lost track of each other but re-established contact when we met again on board a cruise ship sailing on a weekly Bermuda run. My brain cleared and told me that something was not as it should be.

"Well, we were told to break the news to you guys as soon as possible."

Peter said, but hesitated a little as if not knowing how to go on.

"What news? I haven't heard a thing."

I was wide-awake now.

"Well, hmm, well the thing is, we are being taken over, the owners sold out and...... well..."

Peter mumbled.

"What! Taken over, by whom?"

Peter explained, and I found myself listening, but not really listening at all. I vaguely remember Peter haltingly and unconvincingly explaining about a merger of two equals and when he finally finished, I hardly knew what he had said. It was difficult to grasp that we had been taken over and were losing our independence. For a long time I sat on the edge of my bed before I put the telephone down, pondering the consequences of all of this. Then it rang again.

"Hi, it's me again." Peter said. "I forgot to tell you that since you are in port, their President will be coming on board your ship today. He wants to meet with you before you tell anyone about it. His name is Harriman, he will be there around 10 this morning, your time."

I looked at the clock and realized that it was no use going back to sleep, I was wide-awake anyway. There was plenty of time to get myself ready for the meeting, but still being a little dazed, I decided not to lose any more time and get going. I knew this Mr. Harriman from articles in the trade magazines; a legendary figure, short in length but long in energy and dash. It would be interesting to meet him. Deep in thought I walked out of the cabin, almost knocking my steward over. He was just about to knock on the door "to do" the cabin.

"Good morning Gerry, how are you? Busy as usual I

believe."

"Oh yes, I'm always busy Captain."

Gerry had been on board our ship for a long time and was extremely well liked by all of the staff. My cabin was never cleaner and well kept than when he was on board.

"Yes sir, weekly routine. It's Tuesday, and I always take care of the plants in every cabin, doing the fertilizer and such. Tomorrow I change all the beds, then Thursday I do the.."

I waved my hand, because Gerry, if encouraged, would never stop talking. I always have lots of plants in my cabin. One of the first things I always make sure of when a new steward comes on board is checking with him to see if he knows how to take care of them. I do pride myself in having 'a green thumb', but as my schedule is rather hectic at times, I prefer that the steward take care of it on a more regular basis. The next person I ran into was our chief engineer, a short stocky man with an explosive temper. His face made me conclude that his day was not going as planned either. It was deep red and he was mumbling to himself in a language that, I would prefer he do so next to a running ship's engine so that nobody would hear him.

"What's the matter with you? Can't you mind your words a little?"

If possible, he turned a shade redder, with his mouth twisting up at the corners.

"I've called the guy four times and every time he tells me he will be here in 10 minutes. Its two hours now!"

"What are you talking about? What guy?"

"The guy picking up our sludge. I told the office not to go with a new company, but they did it anyway. Why fix something, that isn't broken! Our tanks are almost overflowing with waste oil and that guy was supposed to pick it up this morning, I've been waiting for two hours and he..."

"Alright, I understand, so why don't you call him four more times." I said, deciding that this typical engineering problem, which normally would interest me, was today of lesser importance. I walked into my office, leaving the chief engineer behind me. His mood was clearly not enhanced by my answer. He turned around abruptly and walked off, slamming the door behind him.

I decided to go to the bridge and pour myself a cup of coffee. It was almost 10 by now, and from the wing I would have an excellent view of the pier to see Mr. Harriman arrive. Of course, common courtesy would require me to be at the gangway, but Peter had asked me not to do this, so as not to start any speculation amongst the crew as yet. Sipping from my second cup of coffee I wondered what time my guest would arrive, after all, it was now almost 10.30. Not that it mattered that I was waiting, because watching the activity on the dock below me was not boring at all. There were trucks of all sizes, service vans, forklifts; shifting pallets with luggage and supplies, just one big cauldron of activity.

A car stopped, and I saw a short man getting out. That must be Harriman, I thought, recognizing him from pictures of him in magazines. Short, a thick neck, unruly hair and a crumpled suit, that seemed to be his trademark.

Just as I turned around to go down to meet him at the gangway, taking a last swig of coffee, my eye caught something else. It almost made me choke. Amongst all the activity on the pier, I had seen our chief engineer milling around, still as red as an hour earlier. Now I suddenly saw him charging between forklifts and pallets of food, heading straight for poor Mr. Harriman. What in the world was happening?

"You're late." Even from a distance I could hear the chief yelling. "Three hours I have been waiting for you, and now you show up as if nothing has happened. I'll get you for this.

Where is your truck?"

It was obvious that even Mr. Harriman, with his reputation of always taking the upper hand, did not know what to say. He slowly started to back away, with his mouth open, and showing utter amazement. I saw that he started to say something, but the chief did not give him the opportunity to explain. Helplessly he glanced back at the two men who apparently were traveling with him, as if asking for help against this madman in a boiler suit. The situation did not improve as our chief gave him a shove against his shoulder and backed him up against his car. By now, I think, Mr. Harriman had decided that enough was enough. He ducked another shove and made a desperate run for our gangway, right into the arms of our security officer.

Having stood there inertly, coffee unnoticed dripping from my cup; I suddenly realized that I had better take action quickly.

"Give me a radio fast, don't just stand there," I shouted.

Surprised by my sudden outburst, the officer on the bridge ran away and returned with a Walkie Talkie.

"Gangway, this is the Captain. The gentleman you are holding against the wall is my guest. Release him immediately and show him up to my cabin."

Looking down, I could detect a certain disappointment on the face of our security officer as he released Mr. Harriman from an iron grip. Also, the chief engineer, who by this time had reached the gangway too, in hot pursuit of the 'sludge man', heard my relayed message and his eyes lowly widened. His jaw dropped. This evolved into red- faced embarrassment.

My meeting that morning was off to a difficult start, and I had a lot of explaining to do. Luckily Mr. Harriman turned out to be a good sport and saw the humor of the situation. He smiled thinly and even his aides decided that it was nothing more than a little misunderstanding. I, of course, tried my best to put him at ease, and after about half an hour, we were finally back to normal.

"Mercy, I thought I was going to be attacked. I was late, but not for the reason that your chief engineer thought."

As Mr. Harriman looked around him, he started licking his lips and began to cough.

"Could I bother you for a glass of water Captain, my throat is a little dry after all that commotion."

"Sure, of course, I said. What would you like? I have Perrier?"

"Perrier is fine."

I walked over to my fridge and opened it and found no Perrier. At the end of the cruise, my fridge had not been restocked yet.

"Sorry, I don't have any Perrier, a soft drink perhaps?"

"That's OK, give me a glass of Evian water then."

Knowing that we hadn't had any Evian water on board for months, I shook my head.

"We don't have Evian water either."

"Yes you do." said Jones, one of Mr. Harriman's aides. Amazed I looked at him, how would he know whether we had Evian in my cabin or not?

"We haven't had Evian for months, ran out during ..."

"Well what's that on the buffet?"

A little annoyed, I looked up to my right, but there it was, a big bottle of Evian water, ready to pour. Before I could think further, one of Mr. Harriman's aides rushed forward looking at me with contempt.

"Let me pour it for you. Do you want something too captain?"

"I'll have a Coke," I said.

Still a little puzzled, I helped myself to a Coke while the three of them were sharing the bottle of Evian, which so miraculously had appeared in my cabin.

During the meeting it became increasingly clear that my visitors were not at all impressed with the reception they had received from us so far. Taking over a company was fine, but they clearly had trouble with their first impression. We talked for about two hours, and then Mr. Harriman declared that he wanted to leave, as he wasn't feeling well. He was a little dizzy and his stomach seemed to be upset. His aides also looked a little pale. I felt bad for them. The experience with the chief engineer must have affected them more than I would have thought possible. I escorted them to the gangway wearing a happy face, pointing out the various aspects of the ship as we walked by. After a weak handshake, they left, by now looking ghastly pale.

Back in my cabin, I decided to forget about the whole affair. There was nothing I could do about it. I had tried to handle the situation, as best as I could, but how was I to anticipate the chief engineer's mood and approach.

"It's better I water the plants sir. You told me to and if we both do it, we'll drown them."

Gerry had come into the cabin and looked at me accusingly.

"What do you mean, of course you are watering the plants. I never touch them." I said. Gerry has never been much in awe of any captain, and looking straight into my eyes and shook his head reprovingly.

"Yes sir, you did. I have to warn you though that there was way too much fertilizer in the water. I hadn't diluted it yet."

With a sudden sinking feeling in my stomach, I watched him produce an almost empty bottle of Evian water. Without a doubt, the same bottle I had seen Mr. Harriman and his aides pour their water from. Oh dear, no wonder they didn't feel well. Should I try to call them? But then what?

"Show me the container. What does it say on the label?"

It took Gerry a while to produce the evidence, a green bottle with lots of colorful healthy looking plants on its label. Apparently the manufacturer had thought nobody would be stupid enough to drink from the bottle, as I looked everywhere on the label, but could not find any hint as to what to do after drinking the stuff.

I called Mr. Harriman's office several times that afternoon and finally got through to his assistant. To my great relief, she told me that after not feeling well for a few hours, he was now back at his job but in a meeting. She asked if I could call back later.

I don't know if he ever found out the truth. If not, I'm sure he suspected something. Even now, after more than ten years, he has never again visited a ship when I was on board.

The Chief Executive

Having been a close witness to the enormous growth of the cruise industry over the last 25 years and having seen how companies operate, I am convinced now that to become successful, both at sea and ashore, a company depends on the employees to deliver and on their management for focused leadership.

Some cruise lines, and I would say, these are the lucky ones, have a stable and long lasting group of managers. Others seem to go through CEO's and VP's and ships officers so fast, that a few times over the years I've found myself confused as to who was who and in charge of what at a particular moment. It goes without saying that such a situation creates an almost total break in the chain of communication. I remember a colleague who coming back from vacation found just about all his messages to the office returned as there had been a complete management change in his absence.

There also is another type of company, where the management is stable, but there simply seems to be too much of it. For us at sea, this probably is the most confusing type, as such an incredible amount of instructions and emails are passing ones desk, that it becomes totally impossible to know what has to be taken with a grain of salt and what not. As a matter of fact, we do try to take every message that reaches us, seriously. Sometimes however it's difficult to make the distinction and specially so with American companies which often operate on a first name basis. What to make of a letter from corporate headquarters, often a source of confusing communications in the first place, that is signed simply with 'Jim'.

A specific letter arrived with a bunch of other company mail, stacks of it. It said that Pete would be arriving with his wife to check the ship out, and that John, Kelly and Sue would be joining him. I read it and put it aside on top of a small pile of correspondence I had read already and apprehensively looked at the much bigger stack of mail still unread. As the morning dragged on and I worked my way through, the letter disappeared in the mass of instructions, questions and whatever else people deemed necessary to send me.

I totally forgot about it, and why shouldn't I? The company was full of John, Dick and Harry's and how was I supposed to know them all? They seemed to visit the ship as often as they could find even the remotest possible excuses for, and our homeport was inconveniently close to the office. That is to say, inconvenient for us on board. Each time when the ship was in, a constant trickle of faces passed by me. They all expressed their desire to say hello, talked about a pressing problem I usually had never heard about and undoubtedly used this later on to state that during their ship visit this or that was discussed with the captain, who was sympathetic. Those from the head office of the mother company 5000 miles away were even less real to me and I can't even remember ever having answered any message originating there.

"Pete is coming next week, and I only heard about it this morning!"

An obviously over excited voice yelled in my phone. It was about two weeks later when I answered it, ringing on my desk, expecting a call from the Hotel Manager. On the contrary, it was Bill, my Boss.

"Pete who?"

I answered. For a moment it was quiet, then he continued in a voice, that showed contempt and awe at the same time.

Could it be that there was any person in the whole world who didn't know who Pete was?

"What? Are you stupid? Pete is our CEO and Chairman of the board and…"

Bill continued to recite a host of titles, not entirely unlike those of ancient European royalty.

"And it's only a week until his visit, didn't you receive any communication about this?"

He asked querulously. Suddenly I remembered the letter and guiltily looked at the pile of paper on my desk, which I should have taken care of by now. Instead it was even bigger and going by the distressed sound of the voice on the other side, I decided to avoid the question.

"What do you want me to do? We can go over his cabin and make sure he gets the best service we can give, like the royal treatment."

"The royal treatment?" An apparently totally stressed out Bill yelled in the phone.

"This is Pete, not some kind of stupid king! All these others too, the Chief Financial Officer and…Oh man, the list goes on and on."

"What do you mean, all the others, they said only three."

"No, there will be a lot more."

He squeaked, missing my slip of the tongue.

"The whole board is coming and the ship didn't look all that good to me last time I visited."

"Well, that was last week, and you told me she looked great."

"Yes, I know, but that was for normal passengers, I saw rust somewhere near that thing up front."

I rolled my eyes at the ceiling, not yet caught up in the extreme stress, that apparently had engulfed our Florida office.

"Bill, that was the anchor, those things do rust a little bit at times."

"I better fly over myself to check things out, I'll bring some painters and repair people with me."

A short while later he hung up, leaving me staring blankly at the telephone for a few minutes. What in the world had gotten into him? I decided to walk over to the presently empty owners suite that Pete was going to occupy and to go over it meticulously together with the hotel director. Like me, he had just ended a phone call with his boss, and also like me, he was not caught up in the major panic. His conversation, he told me, had been so chaotic that he still didn't have an inkling who this 'Pete' could be. When I told him, he shrugged.

"Another one."

He murmured. "Well, let's check this cabin, as I have a feeling that pandemonium will break out tomorrow when we arrive in St. Thomas and they come on board to check things over." The cabin, as could be expected on a ship barely six months old, we found in excellent shape.

This conclusion was totally unlike Bill's, who arrived early, even before the immigration officers. Running into the cabin, his hair in disarray, he almost flattened the cabin stewardess against the wall, in his rush to check everything out. After a thorough inspection of about half a minute, he declared the area the disaster he had expected, and looked accusingly at us while pointing to a chair on which the pillow was not positioned according to the high standards the company expected.

I was lucky to be the captain, as for the remainder of the cruise, Bill and his gang of nine workers, were harrying the chief officer to an extent that he practically begged me to slow down the arrivals and departures, as these would be a legitimate excuse for him to be on the bridge and not to be around Bill.

Back in our homeport, with a terminal already buzzing

with excitement and numerous never before seen employees milling around at six in the morning, I heard that Pete would be arriving half an hour before departure. This suited me perfectly fine, as then it would not interfere with my afternoon quiet time. Well, I might as well not have closed my door. By late morning a constant flow of Vice Presidents, Senior Vice Presidents, Presidents and even higher, started to trickle in. Each of them of course had crucially important functions, such as taking care that Pete's shore excursions were well prepared or making sure that his private fax facility was in place; Things which of course could not be left to the crew to handle.

It is common courtesy that when people like Pete arrive on a ship they are welcomed at the gangway by the Captain. In normal circumstances I would receive word of him arriving at the terminal and then make my way down. This time it was different. A good two hours before the scheduled time, Bill came running into my office, where I was playing a little computer game. His mouth fell open.

"What in the world are you doing, what is that?"

"It's called solitaire."

"You have nothing better to do?"

"Well, no, with all these VP's running in and out of here every five minutes, demanding to see me, I'm left with no time to concentrate on normal business, so I might as well kill time…"

Looking at his eyes, I decided to cancel the game.

"So what's the status?"

"We should be at the gangway, Pete might be here any time."

I pointed at my radio.

"I instructed the duty officers to call me as soon as he is within ten minutes of the terminal."

"But what if they miss him, I want you to be at the gangway now, just in case."

"Miss him? With about a million people watching. I'm not going to stand at the gangway for two hours with you."

I contemplated bringing a plastic bag with me, just in case, as clearly he was close to hyperventilating. I refrained from mentioning this, as a joke, any joke would most certainly not be appreciated at this time.

I decided to go along with Bill's request and together we walked to the gangway. To my great surprise, the lobby was filled not only with new passengers dressed in colorful clothes, which by the general public are perceived as the things to wear in the Caribbean, but also with a great number of important looking very nervous men and women dressed in dark business suits. For the next two hours or so, Bill explained who was who and above all, how important everybody was.

Suddenly I heard a gurgling sound next to me and I looked at him.

"There he is, put your cap on!"

"My cap? You don't wear caps inside. I didn't bring it anyway, it's on the bridge."

By that time Pete, his clothes easily matching the most colorful of those of any passenger, had walked up the gangway. Brushing by Bill, he vigorously started pumping my arm with both his hands.

"You must be the skipper." He beamed. "I always loved steam boats. Man, this thing is bigger than they told me."

I didn't have to say much, when we walked to his cabin. Pete kept talking like an excited child and inside I started to laugh. This would be easy, as he behaved very much like any other passenger.

"It smells like wet paint."

He remarked when he entered the cabin, leaving Bill, now number 25 or so in a row of declining importance amongst the Presidents, almost fainted. Pete walked onto the balcony and immediately turned back, white around his nose.

"Pff, that's high! I don't like heights. Don't you have something lower?"

As the ship was fully booked, it took about five minutes to find a family who had saved for many years to book a small cabin on deck number one, to agree that they wouldn't mind being upgraded to the owners cabin. Pete didn't even look twice at his new accommodation and stated that he wanted to see the boiler room. A hastily summoned chief engineer, to his dismay called 'Chieffie' by Pete, took the party down. I smiled and went back to my cabin. This was going to be interesting.

My anticipation was turned into delight when an hour or so later, an upset chief engineer came in and indignantly told me that Pete had been disappointed with his engine room. A clean up because of him had not been necessary, he had told him. He knew that these places always were filled with coal dust and grease and he preferred to see things as they were. He even had asked our chief to show him the 'fires' like he had seen them in the movie 'Titanic'.

The next day, in Nassau, I decided to keep a low profile and not to draw any attention, as undoubtedly, the events would come to me. In this I was right, as around noon, I ran into a harried looking VP, who until now I hadn't seen yet.

"How is it going?" I asked cheerfully.

"Man oh man, what a problem. He wants to see that ship next door and we can't get permission."

"Can't get permission? Who did you ask?"

"We are trying to reach their head office, but they seem to be closed."

"Their head office? Of course it's closed, it's Sunday and it's in England! Calling England for a visit of a ship that's right next to us? What time does he want to go there?"

"In an hour, I better hurry!"

"Hang on, why didn't you ask me to arrange this. I can give them a call, I'm sure it's not a problem."

He looked at me, his mouth open.

"You actually can arrange that?"

"Well, I can try. I'm sure their captain is willing to show Pete around."

The thought that two captains could possibly achieve the complicated goal of arranging a short walk through of one of the their ships, had clearly not occurred to any one of the 25 or so VP's.

"You can actually call them?" He stammered.

"I would be using a telephone, or if that doesn't work, a radio or I could even send an officer across with the request. It's only 25 yards you know."

The other captain as I expected would be happy to show Pete around, and an hour later I found myself walking over as part of a group of about 20 executives. The other ship clearly was ready for us, as her captain, a dignified bearded man in his late fifties was waiting at the gangway. Pete greeted him like he did me the previous day, by vigorously shaking his hand.

"You got a nice boat, skipper! By the way, have you ever been in a bad storm?"

Standing right behind Pete, I saw that my colleague was quite unprepared for this line of questioning. He suddenly lost some of his dignity and stooped a little as he pondered how to answer this one.

"Well, let's walk around your boat, I'm curious how it looks."

Pete continued, unaware of the unsettling effect his words had on the man opposite him. The walk around went well enough. They were on a world cruise, we were told which only had started a few days ago. The type of voyage was very apparent, as almost every passenger we met was elderly and clearly well off; A fact which did not escape Pete's observation either.

"Your passengers are about a hundred times older than the ones on my ship."

He cheerfully announced. By this time however, the other captain had recollected his wits and apart from the fact that only a Captain can talk about 'his ship', he, with a superior smile, remarked that while this fact might be true, undoubtedly they were also a hundred times richer.

"Does this boat rock a lot?"

Again, the other captain looked a little nonplussed.

"Well, every ship rocks at times I suppose."

"Mine doesn't." Pete stated confidently. "We got stabilizers, Right?" he turned around to me.

"Well, yes we do, but it is true, every ship rocks now and then." I answered.

After half an hour, Pete decided that he had seen enough and wanted to get back to his own ship. Walking across the pier again, he pulled me aside.

"We won't be rocking this cruise."

He stated while suspiciously watching me.

"Well, I can't guarantee that, it's January and the weather isn't that stable, but if it happens, it won't be too bad."

"But what about the stabilizers, don't they work? They are the latest models I was told."

I tried to explain the movements of the sea and the ship without discrediting whatever information he had received. Being too specific most likely would cost a few people their job I suspected. Pete clearly was unhappy about my story and once back on board disappeared into a corridor, followed by his entourage.

An hour later, Bill came to my office, a relieved look on

his face.

"Thank God they are gone, it was a good thing you warned him about that storm."

"What are you talking about, what storm?"

"Well, didn't you tell Pete that there was a bad storm brewing down south and that you advised him to get of?"

Bill looked at me in awe. For the first time in all his 25 years with the company he had met somebody who could scare Pete away. I never saw Pete again and as far as I know, he never attempted to make a cruise anymore and we had a quiet voyage after all. Thanks to the big storm brewing somewhere south.

The Stretcher Party

When introducing the senior officers on the first or second night of each cruise, one of those brought to the stage is the ship's doctor. Usually the captain makes light of his position on board the ship. He mentions that the doctor is responsible for a department where everyone prefers a low level of activity or that the passengers should meet him only socially. At this little joke, the audience always voices a polite chuckle and then the next person is introduced. Everybody almost automatically assumes that the underlying facts and reasons that there is a doctor on board, don't apply to them. Like with everything else unpleasant, it always happens to others.

In my mind there is no question at all. The position of the doctor is a very important one. I can imagine that in many cases he carries a heavier load compared to even his counterparts ashore. When a ship is far from the nearest port, he is it! No immediate help from extensive medical facilities. No second opinions and referrals to countless medical experts in every field like doctors on land have available to them.

Apart from the casual remarks to the passengers during an introduction, the medical department is taken very seriously by every crewmember on board. After all, we too depend on it for our health. The vast majority of the medical cases are coughs, flu's, an upset stomach and, although we don't like to admit it, seasickness, minor ailments all of them. Every now and then however it's the real thing and something serious occurs. A cruise ship after all is nothing less than a small town and every issue found there, is common at sea too.

Training for medical emergencies is part of the normal safety drills and a number of crewmembers are selected to assist the medical team in their task. While administering expert medical help is beyond most of the crew, except for the doctors and the nurses of course, there are numerous other tasks that need to be carried out and to which certain crewmembers are assigned. No matter how simple these tasks can be, a certain amount of training is required to act together as a well-oiled machine. After all, what is the use of an organized stretcher team, if there is nobody to simply hold open doors for them or have an elevator ready?

On every ship, crew is assigned to such responsibilities, some carry equipment, others are assigned to keep passengers away and others again have the responsibility to actually carry a stretcher if necessary. They usually are alerted through a ship wide announcement with a location and a codeword. This codeword is used so the passengers are not unduly alarmed.

It's surprising how fast and how professionally a group of people, who ashore would never be called to assist, can react. Passengers in the process of signing for a drink find themselves without their steward, or a lady dancing with a certain officer discovers that her arms are empty, as he suddenly has run off. On one occasion I even found a complete electric drill sticking from a wall, where a carpenter had reacted without delay to the announcement.

The stretcher crews on the bigger ships usually come from one or two departments with enough people to allow for such an assignment allowing for a fairly homogeneous group, but on small ships there is no such luxury. Here they come from every department one can imagine, where there is a person to spare. This of course is understandable, as crew can't have double functions during emergencies.

A big lady with a determined look on her face had stopped

me in a narrow corridor on the pretense of asking her way to the front desk. Now fifteen minutes later, we still stood there and she was in the process of showing me an extensive collection of pictures of her still unmarried daughter. I was desperately trying to figure out how I had gotten myself into this, and more important, how to untangle myself without hurting her feelings too much, when suddenly an announcement sounded through the public address system. It was the code word for a medical emergency with a location, which happened to be a few decks down from where we were standing. While a captain usually has no direct involvement in these emergencies, it occurred to me that utilizing some personal relations skills I could use this to get away while remaining in good graces.

The lady, of course not knowing what the code word meant, continued her slightly longwinded story, adding the fact that her daughter had a good job and excellent prospects. She then winked at me, and suddenly looked crestfallen. I had brought my left hand to my chin to show sympathy, which of course also, without my saying anything, showed a ring on a finger of my left hand.

Just as I wanted to inform her that the announcement we just heard meant some other business for me, her faced changed again and she opened her mouth incredibly wide, her eyes almost popped out of her head and she voiced a piercing scream, which ended in a low moan. Instantly I lowered my hand, taken aback by such an over reaction to a simple ring. Then I realized the expression of horror on her face had nothing to do with me. With a trembling finger she pointed at something down the corridor behind me. At the same time I noticed a loud noise, not unlike that heard in Western movies when a herd of cattle is on the run. Spinning around, I saw a seemingly unorganized motley group of crewmembers running towards us as fast as they could, carrying all kinds of equipment. Without having to think twice about it, I knew that they were the stretcher party, on their way to the location of the emergency. While a group of crew running around like this is certainly not a normal sight, I immediately realized that this was not what had upset the lady. The disturbing part of the whole scene was that the big, profusely sweating, person running in front was our butcher.

When hearing the alarm, he apparently had been cutting fresh T-bone steaks or something like it, as his apron was covered with blood. While this was unusual and frightening enough, easily the most chilling part of the scene was the fact that the man, in his haste to respond, had forgotten to lay down his chopping axe. Swaying it in his left hand, while carrying a first aid box in his right, his mouth wide open, panting for air with the unusual exertion, and six or seven crew running behind him, he really looked like an escaped lunatic.

Squealing, her daughter quite forgotten now, the lady jumped into my arms for protection, almost flattening me against the bulkhead in the process. It took me until long after the crew had disappeared to calm her down. Distant screams, presumably from other passengers, told me that some extra training of the crew during this sort of thing should be the first point on my agenda during tomorrow's senior officers meeting.

Just when I had managed to calm the lady down, I saw the doctor walking down the corridor toward me. He moved at a leisurely pace and had a smile on his face, which bode well for the possible patient.

"What happened?" I asked taking him aside.

"Luckily nothing really. One of our passengers hit the bottle a little too much. He fell down one of the staircases and sort of passed out. He cut his head, but not too bad. I told the stretcher party and the nurse to bring him to the hospital so I can stitch him up. He can't even tell me where his cabin is."

I felt relieved. While patients, apart from the human factor, usually are not that much of a direct concern to a captain, there is always the possibility, in serious cases, of having to divert the ship to a port with a hospital. This of course with all the hassle and possible repercussions of an interrupted cruise.

The lady too, looked relieved, she was on a sane ship after all, with two senior officers right next to her. I looked at her and smiled, but more to myself and about the situation than anything else. The strangest things can happen on a ship, and most passengers would accept just about anything without questions if the crew acted as if it was part of every day business. But then, I reflected, I probably could be made to think the same in an environment so totally different from my normal life as a ship was for most of the passengers.

She glanced at her hands, still holding the pictures of her, for a husband longing, daughter. Her eyes lighted up, my ring temporarily forgotten.

"As I was saying, she is doing real."

In mid sentence she stopped but her mouth didn't close. Again she pointed down the corridor, her face showing fright and horror and even more so than a little while ago. As during my short conversation with the doctor, I had turned and now faced the other direction, I turned around to follow her trembling meaty finger.

"Oh no, not again." I groaned.

The stretcher party was on its way back, again with the butcher in front. His sweating was even worse, his face was contorted and his teeth were bared with the effort of lugging a heavy stretcher along. He was using both his hands now and had his axe stuck under the belt of his bloody apron. The effect

it all had on me, and undoubtedly even more so on every passenger they had passed so far, became even more dramatic
when one looked at the person on the stretcher. Having been
forewarned by the doctor about the patient's having superficial cuts only, at least I knew not to worry too much. To an outsider on the contrary, it could definitely cause trauma. The
man was wildly flaying his arms about, and obviously unaware
of his condition, had smeared himself extensively with his own
blood. On top of it all, he groaned and mumbled incoherently,
adding to the effect of him being the victim of some horrible
attack.

To our good butcher, used to working with fresh meat
every day, the sight was nothing to panic about. The other
members of the party however seemed to be of the same
thought as the passengers they passed. The look on their faces
showed that they all eagerly looked forward to their arrival at
the hospital, where they could get rid of their embarrassing
load and where more able hands could take over.

Having stepped aside to let the party pass, my immediate
thoughts were with the lady next to me, who stood there, trembling from head to toe. She clearly needed some soothing
words. Just as the party had passed and as I stepped back
towards the middle of the corridor, I cast one more look at the
disappearing stretcher crew. I received one more shock.

One of the stretcher-bearers was our garbage facility operator, a very important person on any ship. Not even an hour
ago, he had shown me around his spotlessly clean equipment
on my weekly inspection. Him being a member of this emergency team made a lot of sense. It's as always the same however, with just about every good idea, when implemented one
finds all kinds of never imagined drawbacks. Like the butcher
who, showing his trade with his bloody apron, might, after
due thought, better be suited in another emergency team, some-

thing similar applied to our garbage operator.

I already knew the man was rightly proud of his operation, and not shy of making his position on board known to anybody. But now seeing him from the back running away from me in his coverall as the last man of the team holding the stretcher, his proud advertising was terribly out of place. In his spare hours, and with big letters, he had stenciled the words 'GARBAGE ROOM' on his working cloths.

Even I, who of course knew better, got the immediate impression that some unfortunate victim was carried away in great hurry to be disposed of by a team of lunatics.

It took me the better part of an hour to calm the lady down and after that quite a few other passengers as well. In the end, only the butcher was re-assigned to another less conspicuous emergency team. Our garbage operator was supplied with a set of brand new coveralls and a very blunt message not to write anything on them.

This is the Navy

I remember, that as a young officer, feeling very important and knowledgeable on just about everything, as I had been in the cruise business for three years already, there was one place I had not been yet. That place was Nassau in the Bahamas. More experienced colleagues kept talking about the Nassau to Bermuda run, Nassau to Miami, you name it, and didn't know a thing about it which at times was embarrassing. All this however was a long time ago. Now, after many years in the cruise business, I have been there so often, that at times I feel like being a part of the picture.

It was midmorning and I was standing on the bridge wing, taking a short break, watching the activity in Nassau harbor. I noticed that four gray navy ships were outside waiting to enter the port. Having nothing in particular to do, I decided to wait and watch their arrival, which would most likely be right next to us, as that was the only place in the harbor left with ample space. Although navy ships in general are a lot smaller than cruise ships, this was an impressive sight. Four sleek ships coming through the breakwater, their sailors smartly lined up along the railings.

"Zhese are zhe best ships in zhe world."

I almost jumped. Our senior doctor had appeared next to me and also looked at the arriving ships with keen interest, which now had started their docking procedures. He was a fine doctor and I always felt comfortable with Heinz on board. He had come from Germany originally and in all the years, he had never lost his pronounced accent.

The best ships in the world? Again, I looked at them, this time a little closer. But as far as I could see there was nothing in particular that made them stand out from other navy ships I had seen over time.

"German navy ships, zhere are no better." Heinz stated proudly. "Look at how well zhey stand in line."

He had stretched his arm and with one eye closed he peered at the line of sailors as if putting a ruler along them and nodded approvingly. I had to agree. The disciplined look of the crew on board the other ships outdid that of any cruise ship I had ever seen. But then, I reflected, wasn't that the business they were in?

"I zhink, I will visit them, maybe have some good coffee."

We both smiled. The taste of American coffee had never been to Heinz' liking, and I could visualize him salivating, at the thought of a good cup, made to standards he appreciated.

As it turned out, He did not visit his countrymen. Instead they visited him, or better, they visited our ship and Heinz proudly showed them around.

"Zhis is zhe best ship in zhe world and zhis is our Captain."

I heard him say to a group of smartly uniformed officers when I met them on the bridge a few hours later. They all clicked their heels and bowed their heads, making our duty officer, who was working on his charts, look up, as he had never heard this sound before and thought that maybe some of his instruments were be acting up.

We chatted for a while and some of our officers joined in. I decided that the navy was not for me. Their daily life seemed to be one big exercise and from what they told me about their accommodations I figured they were way too small for my liking. Guiltily, I remembered that we too had a big exercise coming up and that I had not given enough thought of how to carry it out yet.

A few years ago, the company had decided that at least once a year we should conduct a combined drill, with both the ship and the office included. The idea, I had to admit was not a bad one at all, as a major emergency on a ship most certainly would involve the whole company. My problem was more with the slightly farfetched scenarios we were presented with by people who at times seemed to have nothing better to do than coming up with harebrained schemes.

The eyes of the German officers lit up when our Safety Officer mentioned that we too conducted regular exercises and that tomorrow we actually would be doing our yearly big one with the ship at our private island. My beeper went off, and looking at the message I realized I had to run. A cocktail party was waiting and after a hurried goodbye, I sped off. Looking back, that, as far as I can see, was my only mistake. On the bridge the conversation between our Safety Officer, Doctor Heinz and the group of German officers went on. They drank a few pots of coffee and most likely pronounced it undrinkable and from what I understood later, they had a good time.

It was ten o'clock the next morning and I was on the bridge ready to get going with the exercise. Earlier I had received the scenario for it, which I was to follow to the letter. I had started to read it and with every page my misgivings mounted. As usual, there was too much detail, even though I had asked it to be more general. Too many things were thrown in as well. The ship would run aground during a major fire, passengers would panic, we would send out emergency signals and on top of it all, they had thrown in a handful of heart attacks, a major oil spill and an approaching tropical depression. How in the world was I to cope with all that and still make the exercise a success? I knew that back in the office, all work had ceased and everybody and his brother would be in the big conference room. Maybe on the ship too, I should cease all work for the day, I thought gloomily. Like we did not have a few thousand passengers to take care of. The staff captain appeared next to me.

"We better start, if we want to finish this before we sail."

I smiled at him, but he must have taken it as a snarl, as hurriedly he continued.

"So we start with 'running aground' and then a fire breaks out, then a panic and during which the chief engineer reports the oil spill."

He stopped and looked at his copy of the scenario, leafing through it.

"Oh yes, then the heart attacks and then you fall apart, and I take over."

"What? Where does it say that?" I had not seen that I was to fall apart.

He showed me his copy and yes, there it was. I would fall apart on page 26. I had completely overlooked it and with some regret it occurred to me that this was almost at the end of the exercise. It would have been far better if this would happen at the beginning, on page three or four, as that would give me some very quiet time to do some much needed paperwork.

"Let's start. Tell the duty officer that he just ran aground."

It took another five minutes to convince Rick that he had messed up and that we were aground now and what was he going to do about it.

"But we are alongside!"

I heard him exclaiming to the staff captain. I smiled. Seamen are notoriously bad actors and to imagine a grounding, while safely sitting at a dock was stretching the poor officers imagination a little too far. Sourly I noticed that this would be one of the remarks I would make about this exercise. Apart from very few officers, such as the safety officer and me, nobody was supposed to know about the pending drill, a fact, which most certainly would wreak havoc on the ship's services, especially since it was supposed to last a good few hours.

We started, and I must say that initially things went well enough. Unlike normal exercises conducted solely on board, every now and then the office asked for a time out, as someone had to make an urgent phone call or use the bathroom. My remark that during real emergencies, time outs were generally out of the question did not impress anyone. Instead I was lectured on the fact that they were already way into their lunch break, and that would be the next time out. Longingly I looked at my scenario. We were only on page 17, still 9 to go till page 26, where I finally could 'fall apart'.

The telephone rang again. My boss, Bill, was on the phone.

"What are you doing?" He yelled. "What's going on there?"

"What do you mean, just the exercise. We are having a 30 minute time out while you have your lunch."

"My lunch!" He gurgled. "I had hardly taken one bite when the navy called. They are sending all their ships to assist you!"

"What?? The navy? What for?"

"Helicopters too, six of them." Bill continued very upset and not even listening to what I was saying.

"But how can that be, and why? I don't understand. How do you know?"

"They just called us here in the conference room. Some commander told Tom, who picked up the phone as we thought it were you, that they were breaking off their exercise and were responding to your distress calls. It's a mess over here. Tom is calling Norfolk to see what is happening!"

Bill continued for a while and I could hear the confused conversation in his conference room in the background. Suddenly it dawned on me that one of our officers in the initial confusion of this unexpected drill, could have set off real emergency signals instead of sending out a test signals only.

"Mark, over here, right now!" I hissed at the navigation officer, who undoubtedly was responsible for this.

"Check the Epirbs and everything else right now. You set them off, you…" Poor Mark shot off like he was spring loaded and came back a minute later.

"They are alright sir, no real signals were sent!"

"Well, check again, together with the staff captain."

I always try to be as reasonable as possible to the officers, but listening through the phone, to an ever-increasing confusion at the other side, I acted in a little harsher way than I normally would.

On the other side, they again were talking to the navy commander as I could hear. He was launching his zodiacs, as he had us in sight, I figured from the bits and pieces. Open mouthed and uncomprehending, I looked out of the bridge windows. The horizon was at least twenty miles away and nowhere a war ship, or any ship for that matter, in sight. That navy commander must have excellent eyes, and why would he launch zodiacs at such a distance? I did not know what to say, and Bill on the other side would not take my word that there was no navy to be seen.

I was tapped on the shoulder by the staff captain, who with a glimmer of hope in his eyes reminded me that we were closing in on page 26 and that maybe I should lose it now, so he could take over. Confused I stared at him, and then it dawned on me. This must be a part of the scenario unknown to me. Brought in to confuse me so I credibly could lose it. I had to give it to them I had almost gone for it.

"Well, Bill, I'm off now, the staff captain will take over, but I must say, you nearly fooled me."

I didn't hear his reply as I had given the phone to the staff captain. Before I left the bridge wonderfully at ease, I saw him turn white, and he made wild movements with his arm for me to come back.

"The navy really seems to be involved." He stammered. "They are going ballistic over there, total confusion. There seems to be a fleet exercise going on nearby and they are sending four ships. The leader of the flotilla is called 'Brandenburg'."

"Well, let's try to get in touch with them. I can't imagine though what is happening, as they have us in sight, but we don't see them.... Wait a minute...you! Over here..."

Suddenly a glimmer of understanding dawned on me. Hearing the navy ship's name, together with a jerking move our safety officer when he heard it, made me put one and one together.

"What do you know about this?" I harshly asked him.

"Well, hhhmmm, well I... I don't..."

"You! Stay here, don't sneak out, I think you are involved as well."

Our doctor, who for the duration of the break in the exercise had come to the bridge for a cup of weak coffee, had almost managed to sneak away through the safety room. Now both of them stood in front of me, perspiring heavily, Heinz licked his lips.

"What did you do, and why is that navy involved? It's those guys who were here yesterday, isn't it?"

Both of them swallowed hard and piece-by-piece the story came out. As they had talked about us doing our big yearly exercise, while the navy did their own things not too far away, someone had come up with a brilliant idea. Wouldn't it be great to do something together, to make it look even more real?

"Whose idea was it? Come on, tell me."

By the accusing look on the Safety Officer's face, I figured it must be Heinz's.

"Well, zhey do the best exercises in zhe world and I thought maybe we could learn from zhem." He said, his eyes shifting left and right.

"But how in the world did they get to call our head office? They even called directly into our main conference room!"

A blank look in their eyes told me that they were telling the truth when both of them denied any knowledge of this.

"I showed them the ship's telephone numbers and they wrote it down."

The Safety Officer volunteered lamely. They are posted at the GMDSS station here on the bridge. We walked over and I saw that he was correct. The mystery was not solved and I better come up with a good convincing story real soon, as back in our head office there was a bunch of real unhappy people waiting for me to call them back.

"Excuse me, could you please step aside for a moment."

The third officer responsible for the operation of the station, stood behind us. He needed to fill out the radio logbook as to what he had done this morning during the exercise. It took him only a few minutes after which he put the book back. Still mystified I looked at the list with telephone numbers again. Then I looked again...

"What is that?" I roared, pointing at it.

Our mouths fell open. In fat print, a sheet of paper showed every imaginable office telephone number there was, with the emergency numbers at the top.

"But what... how?" With a sudden movement, the safety officer grabbed the radio logbook, standing up against the vertical part of the console. Behind it appeared another list, the one we had seen earlier with the ship's numbers. His mouth opened and he started to laugh, but abruptly stopped when he saw my face and continued with a howl.

"This is outrageous!" He yelled at the third officer. "Why

do you put your log book in front of this list? It's all your fault!"

"My fault? The book always sits there, and so what. So what if it stands in front of that telephone list!" The third officer replied truculently, obviously unaware of the uproar his habit had caused a few hundred miles away in our head office.

It didn't take us very long to see how very funny the situation actually was and also how valuable the lesson of this exercise. Emergencies can never be scripted, as all kinds of unexpected things do happen. On the other hand, I knew that my superiors would not see it this way. To them a scenario was a scenario.

Not exactly looking forward to months of explanations as to what I had done to avoid such an error in the future, I decided that it was best to leave the cause of the incident with a malfunction in the computerized radio equipment.

It has happened to myself a dozen or more times. When calling companies for one explanation or another, a wrong bill or problems with a warrantee on a fridge. You always hear.

"I'm sorry sir, the computer is acting up."

Now after using the same ploy, I know it works. Nobody ever probed me about a further explanation. Thank God for computers!

Memories from a Trunk

There is a saying that knowledge is more important than money, and that it cannot be taken away, once it sits in a brain. Knowledge is power even. I fully do agree with the statement of raising the status of knowledge above monetary values, but at the same time I have some reservations about it not being possible to be taken from a person. Knowledge fades away after a while and it needs refreshing every now and then. New challenges are needed all the time to keep the brain active. The same is the case with the things we see around us, events we witness, they slowly get lost in the blur of life.

Only the big monumental happenings in life are clearly remembered. I saw the 'Great Wall', the 'Taj Mahal' or even the 'Borubudur'. We are able to describe the events and sights in great detail and talk about them with authority during birthday gatherings many years later. The small everyday things however are easily forgotten. What did we see on the road to the 'Taj Mahal' or what did we learn from the Chinese people who live near the wall. People who undoubtedly see this world famous structure more as a nuisance, since it's sitting directly in the way between their village and the pastures, where their cattle is grazing. All these so important but every day things we usually forget about, as they are so normal.

Why should I remember that sunny day during a winter in China when I visited as a navigation officer? We had docked in Shanghai, the most Western influenced city in all China. It was my first visit to this great place, and I was in awe with the sight of the old international settlement, scene of numerous told and untold stories, of fortunes made and lost. I was one of a group of crew, and we were on our way to the Great Wall in an old rickety bus. China was still as communist as could be and we the crew, fellow workers and suppressed proletarians just like the Chinese, were treated ten times better than our guests, who after all were nothing more than capitalist swine.

For lunch, we stopped at a local eatery in a small village. At least that's what we believed it was. Thinking back and looking at some old pictures, I'm not so sure anymore. To me, now, it looked more like a school hastily evacuated for the visitors from the West. Like in many countries, also in China it appears to be the custom that local dignitaries welcome groups of strangers. We all very much appreciated this gesture of goodwill and looked forward to what the elderly gentleman in his drab blue costume would have to say.

It took a while for him to start as he fumbled clumsily with a stack of papers, his ancient glasses bringing back memories of the yellowing photos of some long forgotten family members. His talk was rather monotonous and exclusively in Chinese. It only was a matter of minutes before the attention span of even the most cultural inclined amongst us, started to wilt and it didn't take long before the explorative of our group, and I'm sorry to say that I was not one of them, started to venture out into the hallway in search of excitement. We didn't feel too rude either, as the gentleman didn't even seem to notice. The thought that the same probably happened to him too while addressing his fellow countrymen even occurred to me.

Then a discovery was made, in a room next to us. A wedding was being conducted, an honest to God Chinese wedding! Being the rude Westerners we were, we left the speaker and went to watch the event uninvited. Wasn't this something? Suddenly one of our entertainers, of whom there was abundance in our group, came up with a brilliant idea.

"Let's do a show for them, we got enough of the cast here."

To the bride and groom and the rest of the wedding party it must have been a very strange and totally unexpected sight. One moment you are just getting married, nothing special, and then out of the blue sky a bunch of strangers marches in and starts singing 'New York New York' and that some country you never heard of, somewhere in South America has to stop crying. The performance was a great success and it surely changed our perception of the Chinese, who turned out to be a very generous people. They must have talked about it ever since and possibly for years to come.

"Listen what happened when Grandpa got married."

I however, forgot all about it. Instead I remembered the Wall, a long stretch of bricks and rocks, which rightfully makes people exclaim in awe, but which at the same time is nothing more than that. Now that China has opened up for tourists, and the price to go is low, we can travel there anytime to see it. Is being able to attend a Chinese wedding in a tiny nothing village, and see the wonder and the enthusiasm on the faces of the people when they see an American cast throw a performance at them, not ten times better than seeing bricks? I am certainly not trying to talk down the Great Wall, but even when writing this down, I cannot help but wonder how strangely selective our memory is.

As I said I forgot about it until a few years ago, when finally I had married and bought a house. During my years at sea I had brought together an impressive collection of what I preferred to call artifacts. That my brother, when he saw it all together called it the biggest pile of junk he had ever seen, is not important now. Never having given it a lot of thought, I discovered that my stuff was scattered all over the country. Two antique trunks with my sister, a Chinese table with an uncle who had forgotten it was mine and needed some convincing to give it back, two closets full of boxes at my brother's house, my mother, an aunt.... They all had a share of my booty of years at sea stored away. Now it was time to bring it all together in my new house and enjoy it. While collecting it all had taken me years, convincing family to return paintings from their walls and carrying boxes and crates down numerous staircases, almost was as time consuming.

When finally seeing it all together, the experience was rather shocking. Secretly I had to admit that my brother's description at least was partly correct. Notwithstanding that fact, of course nothing could be thrown away. Every little piece had its story. This I had bought from that not so honest Ali Pouff in Port Said, that from a crippled little boy in Sierra Leone. I saw that the little woodcarving was glued and I remembered it fell off my desk and broke during that terrible storm in the Bay of Biscay.

In a trunk that had come from my mother's house, I found all the letters I had sent her from all around the world. I started reading, and kept reading. They opened up the dark spots in my memory as they told about the small things I had seen. Every day happenings, which only registered for a few weeks and then, were forgotten. Nothing noteworthy had happened, but by going through them I was transferred back in time to Tandjung Priok, Victoria Harbor and Apapa, back in Indonesia, Brunei and Nigeria.

One yellowing bundle of letters was labeled 'World Cruise '78'. Suddenly I was back on my first cruise ship, an outdated steamer, somewhere in the South Pacific. A few postcards, that fell on the floor pinpointed the position a little more accurate and my memory made a leap to Pitcairn Island, that tiny spot in the middle of nowhere, possibly the most remote island on earth; The place of the Mutiny on the Bounty. As a kid, I read the famous book over and over and actually believed it to be a story only; something that was born in the creative mind of a master storyteller. It wasn't until much later that I realized that the drama was real. It had happened and some 50 or 60 descendants of the mutineers still live on that small wind-swept island.

I found an old crumpled picture somebody took. It featured a young one striped officer, with a barefooted gentleman, arms around each other's shoulders. 'The High Commissioner of the Queen and me' it said on the back. I smiled at myself and lost valuable time reading through the whole pile of letters, all about this cruise, while more and more memories surfaced. Digging deeper in the trunk I found other mementoes as well. Beautiful woodcarvings of fish and birds, a walking cane. All made by a variety of gentlemen, all with the same last name 'Christian', carved at the back of each piece.

There was a newsletter too, as if a place with barely 50 inhabitants needed one. Reading it again, the news was like that of another forgotten age. It urged those who had goods to order or to ship, to hurry, as the next mail ship was due in two months. Family news was published and a few articles about how those who had left were doing. How times have changed, computers are pushing us around now and unwanted e-mails ask for immediate answers. In a sudden urge I typed the name of the island into my computer and sure enough, they have a web site now. Somehow this unreasonably annoyed me a little, should not computers bypass such a legendary place.

The people from Pitcairn Island were an unhurried and friendly lot. They came on board our ship to sell their products. No we didn't have to send our guests ashore, too much hassle. There were only two people left on the island anyway, so why bother? They arrived in a great old-fashioned long boat, rowed by the men. They ate our food, drank our wine, sold their crafts. Everyone was happy.

By the time they left, it was late afternoon, the wind had increased and the sea rough. Rowing away from our ship, their boat wildly rocking and foam blowing off the tops of the waves, they sang their farewell song, which left us strangely moved. The island is not exactly a place one plans to visit again in life, so we would more than likely never see each other again. I kept looking at the island till it disappeared below the horizon.

That same cruise we called at two other similarly remote spots, Easter Island with its giant stone statues and Christmas Island, both immensely appealing to the imagination, but only the first one being truly a place of wild fantasies. The latter of the two apparently didn't make too much of an impression on me, as in my letters it was only mentioned as a port of call with the most memorable part being the boat ride back to the ship.

Easter Island however was different. What a grand island that is. I found three thick letters, all about this one place. They kept rambling on about hundreds of statues scattered all over the island. Huge somber faces, cast in stone, some with an eager look, like wanting to tell the world their as yet untold story. Who had put them there, and what natural disaster had made the people who erected them disappear? Reading the letters again, I was not so sure if my mother had even only half understood what I was writing about. Short sentences, fired like gunshots, hopping from one subject to another. For me, however the letters provided insight into forgotten years and how I reacted to new impressions. Sometimes, they were even embarrassing. Was I that naïve?

Suddenly I looked up, it was dark outside and my stomach manifested itself. I had spent the whole afternoon going through not even one trunk. I sighed with anticipation, there were at least twenty to go.

About the Author

Hans Mateboer was born in the eastern part of the Netherlands and ever since he was a small boy, wanted to become a ship's captain. He first went to sea when he was nineteen years old as an apprentice on a rusty old freighter. During his career he sailed under the Dutch, Danish, British and Bahamian flag, on virtually every type of ship there is.

Seeing the decline of the traditional cargo companies, he realized that a drastic career change was necessary and he joined a cruise line in the late seventies. In the ensuing years he was involved with a great variety of activities such as the building of new cruise ships and the organizing and starting up of a new company from the very beginning. He has lived in Italy, France and Germany while supervising the construction of new tonnage. Seeing the small everyday things happen around him, he started to write these short stories for a magazine.

He met his wife Lisa on board and together they live in Charlotte, North Carolina.